It was scary how easy it was.

To show up twice a week to see the kid. To look forward to it. Matt even stayed for supper once. Homemade. Outstanding.

Of course, the widow Corey Madsen smelled good and looked good, too. Matt actually liked her!

And Shorty. Sweet, laughing little Short Stuff.

He was getting so used to her. Always looking for something to buy her. A kitten book here, a cupcake there.

Matt was happier than he had ever been in his life.

And a thousand warning bells were going off inside him.

It was too good to be true. It wasn't going to last. He should have his head examined for letting himself get involved in something that would only bring him grief.

If the kid wasn't his, then what?

And if she was…

Dear Reader,

At long last, summertime has arrived! Romance is in full bloom this month with first-time fathers, fun-filled adventure—and scandalous love.

In commemoration of Father's Day, award-winning Cheryl Reavis delivers this month's THAT'S MY BABY! *Little Darlin'* is a warm, uplifting tale about a cynical sergeant who suddenly takes on the unexpected roles of husband—and father!—when he discovers an abandoned tyke who couldn't possibly be his...or could she?

In these next three books, love defies all odds. First, a mysterious loner drifts back into town in *A Hero's Homecoming* by Laurie Paige—book four in the unforgettable MONTANA MAVERICKS: RETURN TO WHITEHORN series. Then fate passionately unites star-crossed lovers in *The Cougar*— Lindsay McKenna's dramatic finish to her mesmerizing COWBOYS OF THE SOUTHWEST series. And a reticent rancher vows to melt his pregnant bride's wounded heart in *For the Love of Sam* by Jackie Merritt—book one in THE BENNING LEGACY, a new crossline series with Silhouette Desire.

And you won't want to miss the thrilling conclusion to Andrea Edwards's engaging duet, DOUBLE WEDDING. When a small-town country vet switches places with his jet-setting twin, he discovers that appearances can be *very* deceiving in *Who Will She Wed?* Finally this month, *Baby of Mine* by Jane Toombs is an intense, emotional story about a devoted mother who will do *anything* to retrieve her beloved baby girl, including marry a handsome—dangerous!—stranger!

I hope you enjoy these books, and each and every story to come!

Sincerely,

Tara Gavin
Senior Editor & Editorial Coordinator

Please address questions and book requests to:
Silhouette Reader Service
U.S.: 3010 Walden Ave., P.O. Box 1325, Buffalo, NY 14269
Canadian: P.O. Box 609, Fort Erie, Ont. L2A 5X3

CHERYL REAVIS

LITTLE DARLIN'

Published by Silhouette Books

America's Publisher of Contemporary Romance

To R-Two—but you can't read it until you learn how
and you're at least thirty.

Acknowledgments

Special thanks to bookseller Lori Pabón, for getting me
started. To Alma Chambers and Lt. Col. John Chambers and
Major Bill Kiser (ret.) for patiently answering so many
questions—any mistakes are mine, not theirs. To Lee Roberts
for more of the same. And to Barbara Kiser—who is not just a
Friend of the Library, but a friend to pesky writers as well—
Barbara, I really appreciate all your help.

SILHOUETTE BOOKS

ISBN 0-373-24177-1

LITTLE DARLIN'

Printed in U.S.A.

CHERYL REAVIS,

award-winning short-story author and romance novelist who also writes under the name of Cinda Richards, describes herself as a "late bloomer" who played in her first piano recital at the tender age of thirty. "We had to line up by height—I was the third smallest kid," she says. "After that, there was no stopping me. I immediately gave myself permission to attempt my *other* heart's desire—to write." Her Silhouette Special Edition novel *A Crime of the Heart* reached millions of readers in *Good Housekeeping* magazine. Both *A Crime of the Heart* and *Patrick Gallagher's Widow* won the Romance Writers of America's coveted RITA Award for Best Contemporary Series Romance the year they were published. *The Prisoner* won the RITA Award for the historical category as well. *One of Our Own* received the Career Achievement Award for Best Innovative Series Romance from *Romantic Times* magazine. A former public-health nurse, Cheryl makes her home in North Carolina with her husband.

Dear Reader,

In my former career as a public-health nurse, I encountered many lost and abandoned children, and I have nothing but the greatest respect and admiration for the social workers and the foster parents who worked so diligently, often under the worst conditions, to help these little ones find a better life. Unfortunately, there were times when all our combined efforts were unsuccessful.

But now, as a writer, I can have my happy endings at last. I can't tell you how delighted I am that *Little Darlin'* has been chosen for this month's THAT'S MY BABY! I hope you'll want to accompany Corey Madsen, little "Shorty" and Sergeant Matt Beltran to *their* happy ending, and I hope you'll enjoy reading their story as much as I enjoyed writing it.

Cheryl Reavis

Author Note

Once upon a time, there was a young soldier who traveled in a large military convoy all the way from Oklahoma to Fort Bragg, North Carolina. The country was at war, and in town after small town people came out of their houses to cheer the men who would soon stand between them and the worst threat to freedom and democracy the world had ever known. In one particular small town, a little over a hundred miles from his final destination, he saw *her,* and he did the only thing he could do—he scribbled his name and address on a piece of paper and threw it to her. Wonder of wonders, she wrote to him. He wrote back. Soon, he was spending every leave he could get with her and her family. Just before he was sent overseas, they were married....

A fairy tale? No. That's how Mama met Daddy. I've always thought if it wasn't for Fort Bragg, *I* wouldn't be here.

Chapter One

I can't do this, she thought.

Corey Madsen sat on the side of the bed, clutching the telephone receiver so tightly that her fingers ached. She could hear the rain spattering against the windowpanes and the wind in the pines.

She shivered, not from the coldness of the room, but from the emptiness inside her. She hadn't been asleep when the phone rang, but she might as well have been, so deep was her concentration. She had been trying to remember the song—Jacob's song—the sound of his voice, the way he used to sing it when he wanted to tease her, or when he wanted to say he was sorry, or when he—

She closed her eyes, hearing him again, loving him again, living the memory for just one brief moment before it was gone.

Will you always...

Be...true...

It was making her crazy, trying to remember and yet trying to forget.

"You know I wouldn't ask you if I wasn't desperate," the woman on the telephone said. "No one else is available—"

"Mrs. Kurian—" Corey interrupted.

"Mrs. Kurian?" the woman said. "What happened to Lou? We're not going back to surnames at this late date, are we? You and I have been through a lot together—way too much for that."

Corey took a deep breath. "Lou, I'm just not ready to—" She stopped and took another deep breath.

"Corey, I need you to help me here."

"Well, I can't do it."

"I know you miss Jacob. I know you're still grieving. I wouldn't ask you if there was anyone else."

Corey heard all too plainly what the woman didn't say. It had been over a year since Jacob died. And all that time Lou Kurian and her abandoned babies had been left wanting.

But Corey had no desire to try to justify her continued need to mourn. It was her business if she chose to sit in the dark on rainy nights and *not* cry. She just wanted to be left alone.

"Corey, do you remember that time when I was so burned out I couldn't see straight? It was all I could do not to tell somebody to take the job and shove it. I wanted you to feel sorry for me, and you said—do you remember what you said?"

"No," Corey said, anxious now to end the conversation before it was too late.

"You *said*, 'You have to focus on the children and nothing else. Not on their sorry parents and not on yourself. Just them, because it's the only way you can stand it.' You said, 'The children are the ones who suffer if you don't, and they don't deserve—'''

"Don't you understand? It's just me now. I can't do it alone."

"I think you can. If you'd just take this child for a few days…until I can work something else out. I know what I'm asking, but tonight there is no other approved foster home available but yours. It's a baby girl, Corey. She's wet and she's hungry. Her mother abandoned her on the base. The man she says is the father—well, she just left the baby in his car. No by-your-leave, no nothing. And as sad as you are right now, I know you've got what this little girl needs."

Corey closed her eyes, struggling hard to hang on to her resolve. Lou Kurian was good. *Very* good. It had been so long since Corey had felt anything but sorrow—and anger—and if she were honest with herself, she would have to admit that she had wanted to keep it that way.

But she did feel something else now, both an empathy for yet another abandoned child and a sense of obligation to a woman whom she respected and who she knew wouldn't have called if she weren't desperate. Even so, Corey didn't say anything, and the silence lengthened.

"Corey?"

"How old is the baby?" she abruptly asked.

"Well, we don't seem to know. The alleged father denies everything—what a surprise. He doesn't even know her name, much less her age. I'm guessing she's about ten months."

"How did you get involved in this if she was left on the base?"

"Oh, I found out who the mother probably is. There's not much doubt about her identity. At least five people saw her put the baby in the car. She's not as 'alleged' as he is, and she's not in the military. Lucky me, she lives right in my jurisdiction, or she used to. Seems she moved out of her place of residence this afternoon with no forwarding address. And the alleged father, God love him, he's not looking for a new tax exemption. You starting to see the problem here?"

"Yes, I see it."

"And you're going to help me?" Lou asked.

Corey could feel her waiting.

"And you're going to *help me?*" Lou repeated when there was no answer forthcoming.

"Lou—okay, I'll do it," Corey said finally. "But it's just until you find somebody else. I'll get everything ready. You can bring her out."

"Well, now, that's another thing," Lou said. "I was here on the base, teaching a parenting class when the aforementioned alleged father found her—he was doing something here in the same building. I don't have a car seat with me, and he drives a hot little red Corvette, so you know *he* doesn't have one. So could you come and get her? You've still got all that baby stuff, right?"

"Lou—"

"I know, I know. You're thinking, 'Does she actually expect me to come out at this time of night—

in the pouring rain, no less—when she *knows* I don't want to participate in the first place and I plainly said so.'''

"Well, do you?"

"Yes, I do," Lou said sweetly, and Corey couldn't keep from smiling.

"All right, I'll come get her. Where do I go? And please make it someplace easy to find. Everything on the base looks alike to me and nobody there ever gives directions in civilian."

She scribbled the street names Lou gave her on the back of an envelope, but she was still filled with misgivings.

"We'll be waiting for you," Lou said. "I swear it's just until I find somebody else. Just a couple of days at most. Can you hear her crying? Let me get back to her before one of these soldier-types invites her out for a beer. And, Corey, thanks."

Corey stood for a moment after Lou had hung up, still clutching the receiver and trying to summon the discipline and the willpower to do this.

First things first, she thought, finally hanging up the telephone. She immediately went to the small bedroom she and Jacob had made available for the rescued children Lou Kurian brought them. In the three years before Jacob died, it had hardly ever been empty. Corey switched on the nursery lamp and put clean flannel sheets on the crib mattress, mentally checking her supply of clothing to decide if she had anything suitable for a ten-month-old baby girl. If not, they would just have to improvise. The baby would only be here a few days. She had assorted disposable diapers, but no formula or baby food—

and Lou had said the baby was hungry. Corey thought she had enough money in her billfold to buy a can of powdered formula and a few jars of food. If she took along a baby bottle filled with warm water, she could mix some formula and feed the baby as soon as she got there.

She looked around the room. Everything was ready for this little one with no name.

She had long since gotten over prefacing any questions she might have about a situation with "What kind of mother would..." She knew what kind. The kind who for whatever reason—her past, her addiction, her latest boyfriend—couldn't put her child first. Corey tried not to judge, but she didn't excuse. She had known too many good and loving mothers, women who had had emotionally deprived and dangerous childhoods, yet who still managed to take responsibility for the babies they brought into the world and treat them well.

It was still windy and raining when she left the house. By the time she had made a dash into the grocery store and back out to her car again, she was soaking wet. But she was undeterred now, and at least she didn't get lost. Most of Fort Bragg was open to civilians. Sometimes it was difficult to tell where Fayetteville ended and the military post began. The directions were simple enough. Left turn off Bragg Boulevard onto Gruber Road. Continue to the Education Center. Easy enough, even for her.

But just in case it wasn't, Lou had her spotters in position. Someone knocked on the driver's side window before Corey had a chance to open the door.

She rolled down the window slightly.

"Are you here for the baby, ma'am?" an earnest young female soldier asked. She stood waiting for Corey's reply, oblivious to the rain.

"Yes. This is the right place, I guess."

"Yes, ma'am," the soldier said, attempting to open the car door, then standing back as Corey unlocked it.

"She's crying," the young woman said when Corey got out.

"The baby or Lou Kurian?"

The young woman laughed. "The baby. But I think Miss Lou would have joined in, if you'd said no. We found the baby a clean diaper—one of the mothers in the parenting class donated it," she reported further. "And we sent somebody to commandeer a bottle and some milk, but he's not back yet. This way, ma'am."

Corey followed the young soldier into the building, juggling her purse and the can of powdered formula. She slung the diaper bag over her shoulder and tried not to track up the highly waxed floors any more than she could help. Once inside, she knew exactly which way to go. The baby was indeed still crying—loudly.

She found Lou pacing the floor in an empty classroom, the baby girl wailing unhappily over her shoulder.

"Corey, thank God," she said. "Come take this child. I can't do a thing with her."

"Let me get the bottle," Corey said, setting everything down on the nearest desktop. She mixed the formula quickly and tested the temperature on her wrist. It could be a little warmer, but this baby was hungry. "I don't suppose we know if she's allergic to cow's milk or anything useful like that?" she said.

"Nope," Lou answered, handing her the baby. "She didn't come with any instructions. She didn't come with anything at all but what she's wearing—and a blanket. And you can see what kind of shape they're in. I'm just thankful she was left in a Corvette instead of a trash can."

"Telephone, Miss Lou," a different young soldier called from the doorway.

"Let me go see what this is. I'll be right back," Lou said.

Corey looked down at the baby girl Lou had handed her. She was dirty from her clothes and her blanket to her fingernails, her face and hair. There was no "sweet baby smell" about her. And she continued to cry, still resisting Corey's attempt to feed her.

"Easy, easy, baby girl," Corey crooned to her, rocking her gently, trying to get her attention so that she would recognize that food was imminent.

But the baby continued to refuse the bottle.

"What is it, little one?" Corey whispered. "One stranger too many, huh? I know, I know..." She pressed her cheek against the baby's head. The baby didn't feel feverish. And she didn't look sick. She looked hungry.

"If you're a breast-fed baby, we are in *big* trouble here," Corey told her.

"She's not," someone said.

Corey looked around. Another soldier—a sergeant—stood in the doorway. And he was clearly, intensely unhappy.

"How do you know that?" Corey asked, regardless.

"Her mother is a topless dancer at one of the clubs on the Boulevard. Breast feeding would be a serious obstacle to her career."

Corey looked at him. The baby cried louder.

"Are you sure you know what you're doing?" he said.

"Do you want to take over?"

"It's not my kid," he said.

"It's not mine, either," she assured him.

"Look, I'd appreciate it if you could get it to stop crying."

"I'm sure you would," she said, taking a step in his direction. He immediately turned to go. "Wait," she said. "Would you mind taking her shoes off?"

"What?"

"Take her shoes off. The laces are knotted and I don't want to put her down. I think she's in pain. She might be colicky or she might have a really bad diaper rash—or she might be sick. But let's start with the shoes. They look too small for her, don't you think?"

He didn't answer her; he was still annoyed—but he didn't leave. He stood there for a moment, then began to work at untying the knots in the laces. Corey had thought him intense from across the room. Up close, he was absolutely fierce. He was lean and muscular, and he was neither handsome nor ugly. She could see a deep scar over his right eyebrow, and there were numerous scrapes and cuts on his hands in various stages of healing.

He must scare the living daylights out of his underlings, she thought.

She read the cloth name tag sewn above his right breast pocket.

Beltran.

"I'm going to have to cut them," he said after a moment.

And he didn't wait for her to approve the plan.

See the hill, take the hill, Corey thought.

He reached into his pocket—not for a knife, as she expected, but for a pair of nail clippers. The file part of it had been honed until it was razor-sharp.

He cut the laces and pulled off the shoes. The baby stopped crying as abruptly as if someone had thrown a switch.

Corey looked up, her eyes meeting Beltran's. His tough military persona slid away—but only for an instant. He was surprised—more than surprised—and perhaps just a little bit impressed.

I love being right, Corey thought shamelessly. *I absolutely love it.*

The baby was eating vigorously from the bottle now, holding on tightly with her tiny hands over Corey's, grunting as she swallowed. Corey moved away and sat in the chair behind the desk, leaving the sergeant holding the shoes.

After a moment he set the shoes down on the edge of the desk. He seemed about to say something, but a small contingent of privates appeared in the doorway, the young woman who had escorted Corey into the building among them.

"Outstanding, ma'am," she said. "I knew you could do it."

"Actually, the sergeant here did it," Corey said, looking around in time to see him walk away.

"Yeah?" the young woman said when she was sure he was out of earshot. "What did he do? Tell us, ma'am."

"Yeah, tell us," one of the others said. "I can't see Beltran singing no lullaby."

"He took her shoes off," Corey said.

"No way! That baby was crying like that because of her *shoes?*" the young woman said.

"Now we know what to do for you next time you start bawling when you got to take the long walk out a short plane, Santos," one of the other soldiers said to her.

"Shut up, Meyerhauser! I made the jump."

"Booo...hooooo..." Meyerhauser said, pretending to rub his eyes. "Look at me, I'm *crying*—"

"That's enough," Beltran said from the doorway. "Get busy—all of you. Move it."

"Sergeant, yes, Sergeant!" The room cleared noisily—except for Beltran.

"Here," he said, putting a clean, folded towel down on the desk near Corey's elbow. His eyes went ever so briefly to her wet hair and clothes.

"Thank you," Corey said, surprised.

But he was already taking his ramrod-straight, military self out the door.

"Think nothing of it," she said for him. "My pleasure."

He turned back suddenly, and for a moment she was afraid that he'd heard her.

"You want your car started?" he asked. "So it'll

be warm when you take the kid out," he added in
case she didn't quite grasp the situation.

*You know, lady. Cold rainy night? Baby without
much on?*

"Yes—thank you," she said, surprised all over
again. "The keys are in my jacket pocket." She indicated which one with her elbow because her hands
were full.

He hesitated, then walked to her and reached into
her pocket to get the keys, avoiding eye contact the
whole time.

"It's the—"

"I know which car it is," he said.

Yes, she thought. *You would, wouldn't you?* It was
evident, even to her, that he made a point of knowing
all. Seeing all. *And don't you forget it.*

She went back to feeding the baby, looking up
again when Lou returned.

"What was *he* doing in here?" Lou said, looking
over her shoulder in the direction the sergeant had
gone.

"Who, Beltran? He brought a towel. I don't think
he likes wet people dripping rain on his nice waxed
floor."

"He doesn't like babies left in his Corvette, either."

"He's the—"

"Alleged father," Lou finished for her.

"I understand the mother is a stripper or something."

"He told you that? Damn, Corey, I'm impressed.
I had to get that little detail out of the eyewitnesses.
He wouldn't tell me anything."

"Well, he wasn't exactly volunteering information. It was more that he wanted to put me in my place. And you already knew about her, so he wasn't giving up anything."

"So how's our little girl?" Lou said, reaching out to touch the baby.

"I think she's hungrier than what this bottle holds. As soon as she finishes, I'm going to take her on home. It should tide her over until she gets a bath and some clean clothes. Then I'll feed her some more, and hopefully she'll sleep the rest of the night."

"Sounds like a good plan to me. I'll let you know tomorrow when her doctor's appointment is. She seems okay—if you disregard the grunge look. Man, I hate to see a dirty baby."

"So how do you know Beltran's the one?" Corey asked, more curious than was really appropriate. Fortunately, even as professional as she was, Lou didn't object to a little gossip.

"The mother left a verbal message with one of the eyewitnesses. She said, 'Tell Beltran it's his turn.' His name, his car—ergo, his baby."

"And his subsequent unbounded glee."

"Nah," Lou said. "He's *always* like that. He's a jump master."

"Intense," Corey said.

"Intense? Corey, my child, of course he's intense. You got to be forceful if you want people to go jumping out of a plane just because you tell them to. Now, he's somebody who *needs* a baby—no, I'm serious," Lou said when Corey raised both eyebrows. "That's about the only thing I can think of that might loosen him up. I've dealt with him before. He was a big help a few times with some of his soldiers who lived off base—family crisis stuff. It kind of surprises me that he won't own up to this."

"Maybe she really isn't his."

"Well, that's his story and he's sticking to it. Anyway, he's on his way to the Balkans for six months— possibly nine, so I guess it doesn't really matter. He couldn't look after her even if she was his. I'm almost a hundred percent sure the woman who left the baby in his car is the real mother, but until I can verify it, this little girl is officially a Jane Doe. God, I'm tired. Let's get out of here."

The baby languished contentedly in Corey's arms now, not quite asleep. Corey stood and, with Lou's help, began to gather up her purse and the diaper bag, the can of formula and the shoes.

It was raining still, and she covered the baby as best she could with the dirty blanket and the towel Beltran had brought.

"Here we go," she said to her little bundle, hurrying to the car behind Lou, whose job it was to open the passenger side door.

"Corey, you're a good woman," Lou said as Corey buckled the baby into the car seat.

"I'm a sucker for your sob stories, is what I am," Corey assured her.

"Same thing," Lou said. "Drive carefully. See you tomorrow."

The car was comfortably warm, and the baby had fallen asleep in spite of the dash out into the bad weather. As Corey began to back out, a soldier came to the front door of the building and stood watching.

Sergeant Beltran.

He stepped out into the rain, intercepting her car when she was about to drive away. Corey rolled down the window, expecting to be accused of absconding with the towel.

"Here," he said, shoving something into her hand. "Buy the kid a new pair of shoes."

Chapter Two

I can't get out of the damned orphanage, Matt Beltran thought yet another time.

Somebody was crying in the dark and had been for a while.

How many times had he lain awake and listened to that sound when he was a kid at Holy Angels? Fifty? A hundred? He had thought he was doing a really intelligent thing when he enlisted in the army. All he had done was trade one orphans' home for another.

He had determined where—and probably who—the crying was coming from, but he made no attempt to intervene. He stood in the mud outside the tent in the cold wind, wishing he still smoked. He was too agitated to sleep. Peacekeeping in a country that had essentially self-destructed was getting on his nerves.

It seemed as though nothing was alive—unless you counted the enmity among the ethnic groups. That flourished unchecked. And what little was left of the infrastructure was obsolete and eerily misplaced in time. The countryside, the towns, looked like something from 1940s news footage—even without the destroyed roads and buildings.

And the crying wasn't helping.

He was tired of being muddy and cold and wet. He was tired of trying to chase down some informant's lead to an ever-elusive cache of weapons. He was tired of MREs—meals ready to eat—and powdered soup. He was just plain tired. He didn't like to think about what he might be willing to do for an actual apple, a piece of lettuce or, God, yes, fresh strawberries. He needed some minor vice—a pack of cigarettes, or better yet, a good party to take his mind off his troubles, one full of loud music and booze, and women with big hair and big breasts and no inclination whatsoever to do the will-you-respect-me-in-the-morning dance. Unfortunately, there was no wild partying here. Just the occasional VIP visit, during which some eager and personable young soldier got to go on camera and give the folks back home the sound bite of the week.

He turned abruptly and headed for the mess tent. Coffee wouldn't hurt. He was cold and he wasn't going to sleep anyway. He could hardly see where he was going, and he had no idea if the current blackout was the result of another failed generator or some other, more ominous reason.

The wind carried the sound of the crying with him. He stepped inside the mess tent and fumbled along in the darkness until he found the coffee urn. At least the coffee was hot.

"Who the hell is that bawling?"

Matt recognized the voice as Burke's, another non-com.

"It's one of mine," he said, sitting down at the same table with his coffee.

"Damn female so-called soldiers—"

"It's not a woman."

"Yeah, right."

"It's not a woman," he said again.

"So what's wrong with *him*—and I use the word loosely. Besides missing his mommy and daddy and freezing his ass off in this mud hole, I mean."

"I didn't ask him."

"You didn't ask him," the other man repeated.

"That's right."

"This is the New Army, Beltran. We got to hold their hands. You know—be sensitive and tactful-like."

"He'll tell me if it's something I need to deal with." He could feel the other man looking at him in the dark.

"You want to go shut him up then? He's starting to get on my nerves."

"Get over it," Matt said, in spite of having the same complaint himself. He abruptly ended the conversation by getting up and walking away.

The other man swore, and Matt turned back to him, waiting, saying nothing but ready to defend his authority if he had to. His people were just that— *his*. He took the job of looking after them seriously, and he didn't want any unsolicited advice as to how he should do it. The kid who was crying was a good soldier, and bawling in the dark—on his own time—wouldn't change that.

"You're a crazy son of a bitch, Beltran, you know that?" the other man said.

"Excuse me, Sergeant Beltran?" somebody said in the doorway. "Sergeant?" he said again when Matt didn't immediately answer.

"Who is that?" Matt said finally, turning his attention to the intruder who was noisily making his way forward, and about to walk into a table.

"It's Wilson, Sergeant—ow! I've been looking for you. I brought your mail," the young soldier said, holding it out to him in the dark. It hit Matt in the chest.

"I can get my own mail, Wilson," he said, shoving it aside.

"Sergeant, the lieutenant says it has come to his attention that certain correspondence belonging to you has been lying around unclaimed. And he says he don't like that—especially if the letter looks like something that's going to cause him a problem."

Matt frowned and took the envelope Wilson still held out to him. He hadn't bothered with his mail, because the kind of things that followed him to a place like this were never worth the effort. The consensus of opinion among his fellow noncoms was that he might get some "real" mail if he ever hooked up with a woman for longer than one night. The real truth in that assessment was that he deliberately chose not to get to the letter-writing stage with any woman. That, too, wasn't worth the effort. He preferred to keep his life simple. No complications. No unnecessary aggravation. He didn't want to string himself up emotionally. He didn't want to live for mail call or drive himself crazy wondering what the girl he left behind was doing to amuse herself in his absence. He had learned a long time ago not to hang his hopes on anyone but himself. He had spent too many hours standing by an orphanage window, earnestly waiting for his fantasy family to come and take him home. The family—fantasy or otherwise—never showed, and he had resolved never to let himself become that pitiful again.

He gave a sharp sigh. He had no doubt that regardless of his wants, he was about to be royally aggravated.

The envelope was heavy on one end. He held it up, but it was too dark for him to read the return address. He folded it and stuck it into his jacket pocket.

"You're not going to open it, Sergeant?" Wilson asked.

"Wilson, you are pushing your luck here."

"Yes, Sergeant. Sergeant, the lieutenant is going to want to know if you opened it. The lieutenant says—"

"Hold this," he said, giving Wilson his coffee in the dark. He took the envelope out of his jacket pocket and slowly, noisily, tore off the end. "You hear that, Wilson? You tell the lieutenant I opened it." He stuffed the envelope back into his pocket and took back his coffee. "Now beat it!"

"Yes, Sergeant!"

"Who you got knocked up now, Beltran?" Burke said, snickering in the wake of Wilson's equally noisy departure. "You haven't been fraternizing with the civilians again, have you? Nah, you got to have a Corvette to do it and you ain't got one over here—"

Matt left him talking, and crossed the compound in the dark. He wasn't going to think about the baby girl Rita Warren left in his car or the subsequent amusement it had provided the entire division. Ready Rita, the self-proclaimed exotic dancer, firmly dedicated to putting a big smile on a soldier's face— usually. The sad little girl who collected china tea- cups and who wanted to be a Vegas showgirl or a movie star. Yet another orphan in his life.

But the kid she'd dumped was *not* his. He would remember how it happened if she was. Surely to God, he'd remember *something*. But he didn't. The only thing he recalled was a remote—very remote— possibility. A night when he'd been so messed up that he might have taken Rita up on one of her many offers. But that was all. A possibility. Maybe she had given him a window of opportunity. The only prob- lem was that he had no idea what he had done with it.

He had to wait until the next afternoon before he could actually open the envelope and read the con- tents. It was impossible to find a place to do it where he had any privacy. He kept looking over his shoul- der and at the return address. The Department of So- cial Services—Lou Kurian specifically. What the hell did Miss Lou want—as if he couldn't guess.

He eventually dumped out the contents, a second

envelope that had been taped shut, and a two-page letter.

He began to read the letter first, searching for the ever-present bottom line. It didn't take him long to find it.

...the foster parent with whom the child was placed always keeps detailed progress notes on the children in her care, to be shared with the potential custodial parent or guardian at the department's discretion. Because you have expressed some interest in the welfare of this still unclaimed baby girl—

He what?

Oh, yeah. Money for the shoes.

Well, they were *wrong!* he thought, crumpling the letter and drawing inquisitive looks from the passersby. He was not this kid's potential anything, and nobody—*nobody*—was going to manipulate him into saying he was. He knew firsthand that Lou Kurian was the Iron Mike of social workers. She did whatever was necessary, and she took no prisoners. But she wasn't going to win here—not with him. And neither was the foster mother, no matter how good she looked soaking wet.

Still, he smoothed out the letter and stared at the second sheet. It was handwritten—by the foster mother, he supposed. Very neatly done. Very A-student. If this was the same woman who had picked up the kid at the base, he didn't know that he was particularly reassured. He had heard some of Lou Kurian's side of the conversation that night, and from what he could tell, she had played hell trying to get the woman to even take the baby.

He read the medical report from the doctor. The kid was a little small proportionately—slightly below the fiftieth percentile—whatever the hell that meant. He noted the kid's weight and height, but it didn't tell him anything about percentiles. He read the description of her appetite and food preferences, and he tried not to smile at the part that said she was a good eater except for her firm conviction that the "only good green bean is a dead green bean."

Hoo-ah! Way to go, kid.

He continued to read, surprised that he was so interested in what the foster mother had written.

She has the new shoes, which I believe she'll take for an actual walk very soon now, because she's already very good at standing alone. There was some money left from your donation. It was used to buy her a hat—see picture. We tried on several. This one was definitely "her."

He opened the second envelope. A snapshot fell out. He turned it over. It was a close-up of the baby girl. The hat was white, soft and fuzzy like a blanket. It looked like a New England whaler's sou'wester with the front brim turned up and held in place with the same kind of fuzzy white bow. It had earflaps and it tied under the chin.

And what a face. What a pensive...beautiful... little face.

She looked gravely into the camera, neither smiling nor about to. Just looking, her little mouth slightly askew, her eyes wise and not sad so much as infinitely understanding and forgiving.

This is just how it is and it's okay, she seemed to be saying.

He kept staring at the picture.

And staring.

This is not my kid, damn it!

He put the photograph down and immediately picked it up again.

This is not my kid....

Chapter Three

Corey hurried to intercept Lou Kurian before she could knock on the storm door. The day was sunny but deceptively cold, and Lou stood on the porch shivering in the sharp wind.

"Help," she said as Corey stood back to let her in.

"You couldn't find another foster home," Corey said, anticipating that the reason for Lou's visit had nothing to do with wanting to get out of the cold.

"I couldn't find another foster home," Lou agreed.

"And you want me to keep her awhile longer."

"And I want you to keep her awhile longer," Lou said dutifully.

Corey looked at her for a moment. "Okay," she said.

"Okay? You mean it?"

"I mean it."

"Bless you," Lou said. "Bless you, bless you, *bless* you!"

Corey smiled at yet another of Lou's benedictions, then gave a small shrug. "It's…working out better than I thought. It's not all that different, really. I'd forgotten that Jacob was always busy with something at the church and I did most of the hands-on stuff anyway."

"Whatever the reason, I'm telling you right now, you just moved up on the list of beneficiaries in my will."

Corey laughed, because neither of them were exactly rolling in money. "Want some coffee? The baby is asleep."

"Thought you'd never ask. So how's our little project coming?" Lou asked, taking off her coat and draping it over a kitchen chair.

"I was about to ask you that."

"Well, the mother hasn't turned up, and there's no word from the sergeant. I told you I sent him the picture and your report."

"You didn't really think you'd hear from him, did you?"

"Of course I did. I told you, he's softhearted. And sensitive, too."

"Oh, please. Lou, I've met the man."

"But you didn't get past the big tough warrior thing. I'm telling you, he *cares*."

"Uh-huh," Corey said, pouring the coffee.

"Didn't he buy that baby a pair of shoes?"

"Yes, but she's probably *his* baby."

"His or not, the kind of men I usually have to deal with won't buy food—much less shoes—even when they *know* the kid is theirs. Beltran is a refreshing change."

"So what are you going to do? Browbeat him into acknowledging paternity?"

"I never browbeat," Lou said, feigning shock at the mere suggestion that she might resort to anything so heavy-handed. "All I did was send him the picture and your report. If I don't hear from him, I'll just wait until he gets back from the Balkans. If he still doesn't get in touch with me, then I'll go see him. We'll have a little exchange of information, and *then*—if he's stubborn enough to resist my gentle persuasiveness—maybe I'll bully him a little bit, just possibly raise my voice. I'm cutting him plenty of slack here. I know finding out you've possibly got a kid takes some getting used to. I'd expect him to be a little huffy about it at first. And maybe he's not the father, but that little girl deserves a shot at identifying the man who made her. For child support, if nothing else. I intend for him to know everything there is to know about this baby, so he can come to an intelligent and honorable decision. Trust me, Corey, it's a lot easier to reject a hypothetical child than it is to reject one you've actually met."

"Or gotten pictures of," Corey said, sitting at the table with Lou.

"Or gotten pictures of," Lou agreed. "Wasn't she the cutest thing in that hat?"

"She still doesn't smile, though," Corey said.

"Never?"

"Never. She's come close a time or two. That's

part of the reason I think I should keep her. I don't want to make her feel secure and then turn right around and hand her off to somebody else. If she's going to trust me enough to laugh at my silliness, then I owe her something a little more long-term."

"Hoo-ah!" Lou said, toasting her with the coffee cup.

Corey shook her head and smiled. "What does that mean, anyway? 'Hoo-ah.'"

"Corey, how could you possibly have grown up in this area and not know that?"

"My mother wouldn't let me hang out with soldiers," Corey said simply.

"Or Jacob, either, I expect," Lou said, making Corey smile. She appreciated the way Lou had no hesitation about mentioning Jacob's name. It left Corey free to talk about him, as well, with none of the awkwardness she felt with other people.

"So what does it mean?" she asked again.

"As I understand it, it means everything but 'no.'"

"Handy," Corey said, sipping her coffee. "If you can read minds. Do you know when the sergeant will be back?"

"Oh, yes. And he'd better have on his track shoes if he's planning on staying ahead of me—whoa, look at the time! Got to go. I'm just going to take a peek at the baby and then I'm out of here."

Corey sat at the table with her coffee and waited for Lou to return. She was tired, but pleasantly so. The truth of the matter was that both she and the baby were thriving. She had no time now to sit in the dark and try to conjure up memories of Jacob.

She concentrated all her energy on taking good care of this child, on keeping her fed and clean and dry, and on trying to coax her solemn little face into a smile. As serious as she was, Beltran's little girl—and Corey had to work hard *not* to think of her as that—was delightful in all respects. She was cautious but interested in everything going on around her. And she loved anything with pictures. She would sit and quietly turn the pages of books and magazines, patting the ones that pleased her with no inclination whatsoever to crumple or tear, knowing immediately whether or not they were upside down.

Corey's mind went to that rainy night more than a month ago when she'd first met Sergeant Beltran and brought the baby home. She thought about him more often than she would have liked to admit. She even worried about his safety in the Balkans—on the baby's behalf, of course—and had taken to leaving the television on the cable news channel, because that was the only place where peacekeeping in that area was ever mentioned. But she wasn't as optimistic as Lou was that anything would come of her campaign to coerce the man into admitting paternity. She did agree on one point, however. This little angel deserved a shot at identifying the man who had made her.

Corey gave a quiet sigh, wondering yet another time if that man was Beltran.

"She's still asleep," Lou said in the doorway. "That child really cleaned up good, didn't she? If she is Beltran's kid, he's not going to stand a chance."

Actually, Corey thought that the marked improvement might very well go unnoticed, but she didn't say so. Money for shoes wasn't necessarily the harbinger of a lifetime commitment. No one knew whether Beltran would even see the baby again, though Corey had no difficulty imagining Lou Kurian dragging him by his ear for a supervised visitation.

"You haven't found out her first name yet, have you?" Corey asked.

"Nope. Not a clue. We've got a search on for her birth certificate, but who knows if she was born in this county or even this state. Or if the mother is using her real name now. Or if her name has changed since she had the kid. It all takes time."

"Don't any of the people her mother worked with know the baby's name?"

"No—and none of the neighbors, either. I guess knowing a child's name isn't high on the list in some places. Or they just don't want to tell *me* anything."

"If I don't find out what it is soon, she's going to think her name is Shorty."

"Shorty?"

"Old Mr. Rafferty across the street calls her that—and he's got me doing it."

"Well, it kind of fits. She's certainly not overly tall at the present."

"Yeah, well, 'Shorty' is going to look pretty odd on her wedding invitations."

Lou was smiling and continued to do so.

"What?" Corey asked.

"This is more like the Corey I used to know," Lou said. "I'm glad. I've kind of missed you."

Corey didn't know what to say to that, and she

looked away. She *had* been feeling better of late—and increasingly guilty, as if her long-delayed return to the world of the living was somehow disloyal to Jacob and diminished what she had felt for him.

"Well, no rest for the wicked," Lou said abruptly. "And the righteous don't need it. Thanks for the coffee. Call me if you need me. I'll let you know when the sergeant blows into town again."

I'm not sure I want to know, Corey thought. Beltran was entirely too...disquieting. All that barely contained military *machismo*—or whatever it was—was a bit much for her. She had never been around a man like him. Never.

But once again, she didn't say anything.

The baby was starting to fuss, and Corey went to get her, carrying her into the kitchen in time to hear the tail end of a news report about the Balkan peacekeeping forces—American soldiers caught in a deadly crossfire.

Matt took the Corvette for a test drive to no place in particular, though he was in a big hurry to get there. He sped along, faster than he thought he could get away with, out of Spring Lake on Route 87 to Pineview, radio blaring all the way. He abruptly took a right on Route 27 to Lillington, intending to head back to where he had started on Route 210. But it wasn't the performance of the car he was testing. It was its ability to take his mind off his troubles one more time. He cranked up the volume for the Rolling Stones's rendition of "Play With Fire," losing himself in the music, letting certain lines of the song underscore his carefully maintained indignation at

being shotgunned into fatherhood. Lou Kurian and
the foster mother were playing with fire when they
played with him. And they had played with him just
about all they were going to.

He had been back in the country for nearly a week
before the second letter from the Department of Social Services arrived. He had been anticipating another one—had expected Wilson to hand deliver it
the entire time he'd been in the Balkans. But that
letter must have gone to his commanding officer instead—which was why he was suddenly sent back
here *way* ahead of schedule. Miss Lou had jacked
him up and left him dangling. She had deliberately
let him think he was home free on this thing before
she jerked his chain again. It wasn't going to work.
He'd had weeks to think about it, and he was convinced now. Absolutely, positively convinced. The
kid was not his.

So why are you still carrying her picture?

The thought ambushed him from out of nowhere.
Okay, so he still had the picture. He could feel it
right now in his left breast pocket. And not only was
he still carrying it, but the day after he had gotten it,
he actually paid one of the company's loan shark-
slash-entrepreneurs a dollar for a zippered plastic bag
to put it in. He hadn't wanted anything to happen to
the picture in the event that he ended up facedown
in the mud in that godforsaken place. Inexplicably,
he didn't want anything to happen to it now. He'd
had all kinds of opportunities to throw it away—the
way he had thrown the Social Services's letters away.
But he hadn't. Every time he'd been on the verge of
doing so, he had looked at the little face, and he had

kept the picture, just as he had kept the handwritten report from the foster mother.

"Below the fiftieth percentile."

"The only good green bean is a dead green bean."

I am not going to be railroaded into this! he vowed.

The traffic ahead of him began to slow and then to bottleneck. He couldn't see the reason for the delay, and he crept along, his impatience growing. Eventually, he found his way back to the trailer park where he lived when he didn't have to be on base. He rented a trailer in the last row on the back side, a choice spot on a slight rise near a stand of tall pines. It was quiet there—maybe a little cooler in the summer. He liked it. He was always glad to come back here.

But if the drive to nowhere had been even remotely beneficial, he couldn't tell. He was still wound tight, and the vehicle that immediately pulled into the driveway behind him didn't help. He looked over his shoulder in time to see Lou Kurian open the car door and get out.

He swore under his breath. She had his car blocked in. As much as he wanted to, he couldn't make a run for it—not that it would do any good. Miss Lou was notorious for her tenacity. He had no choice but to talk to her. He sighed heavily. There was no point in delaying the inevitable.

He got out; she stood by the front steps like a pumped-up tackle just dying for the quarterback to hand off the ball. He waited for her to stop looking at him and get to the point, but she didn't say anything. He could hear the wind sigh quietly in the pines and children playing off somewhere to his left. He could hear country-western music coming from the nearest trailer, smell their supper that included fried onions and baked bread.

He waited some more.

Nothing.

"What?" he said finally, and she smiled.

"Sergeant Beltran," she said sweetly. "I thought you'd never ask. I'm here—"

"It's not my kid," he said, heading her off.

"Are you—"

"How many times do I have to say it? It's not my kid!" he said loudly.

"Forgive me, but given the circumstances, it looks a lot like it is your kid," she said.

"I can't help that."

"Why would Rita leave the baby in *your* car?"

"Ask her," he said.

"I would…if I could find her. Which is the whole point of my being here—"

"Look! I want you to back off! I am not the guilty party here!"

"So there's no way that child can be yours?"

"None."

"You and Rita Warren never did the deed? She just picked you out for no good reason whatsoever."

"Maybe she likes Corvettes."

"Or maybe she likes you. Maybe she picked you because she thought you'd do the right thing, regardless. Lord knows, that's all *I* want. For you to do the right thing."

"It's not my problem, damn it!"

"No, it's mine. That's why I'm here."

"What do you expect from me?"

"I expect better than what I'm getting, Beltran—especially with your background. You know what it's like not to have a family. You know what it's like to live on the charity of the state or the church. What would you have given when you were a little kid to have somebody step up and claim you?"

"Look, I'm not the fatherly type, okay?"

"Rita must have thought so," she said, and he laughed.

"Yeah, and we all know what an outstanding judge of character Ready Rita is."

"Well, I can see why she would arbitrarily pick you—if that's what she did."

He didn't say anything. They weren't getting anywhere with this discussion, and he moved to go inside.

"You don't want to see the baby, then?" Lou said.

He still didn't say anything.

"So you're done with it, is that right? You've handed this baby over and we at Social Services can do whatever we want to with her—declare her a ward of the state and put her up for adoption, put her in a home. You don't care because you're absolutely, positively sure you are not that little girl's father."

"I can't help you, Miss Lou."

"Okay, fine. That's it, then. I've always thought you were a decent and honorable man. I still do. I'm not even going to get the powers that be to lean on you to have the paternity test—and you know I can. This baby deserves a parent who wants her. I'm going to do everything I can to find her one. I'm sorry it isn't you, Beltran. Believe me, it's your loss."

She turned to go. He waited until she opened her car door.

"The kid is okay?" he asked.

Lou Kurian looked at him, then shrugged. She was trying to outmaneuver him. She was deliberately trying to worry him. He recognized that immediately, but he still wanted to know.

"Is she okay or not?" he said more forcefully.

"What do you care?" Lou said. "She's not yours."

He swore, and she held up both hands.

"Sorry," she said. "I'm upset, and I'm taking it out on you. Sometimes I lose patience with—" She didn't go on. She turned and got into her car.

"Is the kid okay or not?" he asked again, following after her.

"She doesn't smile, Beltran," she said. "She is the sweetest, gentlest little thing in this world—but she doesn't smile."

She started the car.

"Wait," he said. "I could...see her, couldn't I? Even if I'm sure I'm not her old man. She was left in my car. It's not like I'm not interested in what happens to her—"

"No," Lou said. "We're not playing that game, soldier. If you want to see her, it has to be because you think there's a chance she *is* yours. I think she's had a hard time—who knows what that little thing has had to put up with? My job is to protect her, if I can—not give her more grief and confuse her with revolving-door father figures."

"Aren't you doing that already? With the foster father or whatever you call him?"

"There is no foster father in her case. The foster mother is a recent widow. There is no male in the household—"

"How recent? Are you sure she's fit to take care of the kid?"

Lou frowned. "Fit? Of course, she's fit—"

"Is that the same foster mother who came to the base?"

"Yes."

"She didn't want to take the baby, did she? That night you called her."

"No," Lou said patiently. "She didn't. But it's worked out fine. Sergeant Beltran, I am very glad you're concerned about this little girl, but I need more than that. I need more than my rapidly fading hope that some day you'll get your head screwed on straight about this thing. If you think there's the slightest possibility that that baby is your daughter and you're willing to do something about it, you let me know. I'll arrange for you to see her."

She didn't give him the chance to say anything else. She backed out of the yard and drove away. He stood there for a while after she'd gone, until he could hear the wind in the pines again and the country music. He took a deep breath. Miss Lou, God love her, had made her point loud and clear. It was entirely up to him. He was off the hook as things stood now, and he could leave it that way or he could—

What? Suppose he did step up and take a paternity test, and then the kid *wasn't* his? He'd look and feel like a fool. It wasn't as if he'd gone looking for Rita just so he could hook up. What was he supposed to do when he didn't remember anything?

Not true, man, he thought. The truth was that he didn't *want* to remember.

But sometimes the memories came flooding back anyway, jagged, broken bits and pieces, falling into his mind, in spite of everything he did to bury them.

He could almost hear the song. ''Bad Company,'' the signature tune of the incorrigibly bad-assed, the one that always precipitated fits of nostalgia for his good old, right-out-of-basic days.

Warriors!

Bad Company.

Who kept playing it?

I did. I kept playing it.

Over and over.

Dead soldiers.

Lined up on the bar.

Dead soldiers.

Lying on the tarmac.

I should have been there. I should have been there!

Soft breasts pressing into his back.

Rita. Ready Rita.

Go away, goddamn it!

Matt. Come on, Matt. You're going to be all right....

But he wasn't all right. Not then. Not now. He turned abruptly and went inside the trailer, then looked around as if he'd never seen it before. It wasn't home. He had no home. He had never had one. He didn't need one. All he needed was a little peace, and he didn't have that, either. He had been to the so-called grief counselor. Taken the pat on the head and the very earnest assurances that nothing was his fault. Fit for duty. Hoo-ah!

The counselor just didn't get it. No amount of talking could make the guilt go away. No matter how many group counseling sessions he endured, one simple fact remained. Good old Sergeant Beltran was supposed to have been there—and he wasn't. It didn't matter why. It only mattered that it was his duty and he hadn't done it. He understood that fine point perfectly, just as he understood that he had been backed into a corner over this paternity thing. And if he wasn't very careful, sooner or later he would be giving Lou Kurian a call.

Chapter Four

"Is the baby over her cold?" Lou asked.

Corey shifted the receiver to her other ear to avoid a tug-of-war with the budding phone-talker she carried on her hip. "Yes, she's fine. Why?"

"It's a go with the sergeant."

"You're kidding. When?"

"Ho-doh!" the baby said, reaching for the phone. "Ho-doh!"

"That's right," Corey said, smiling at her. "Hello! But this time it's for Corey—what did you say, Lou?"

"I said this afternoon at two, if you can make it. I know it's short notice, but he just called."

"I thought we'd given up on him."

"Well, not quite. Just enough to annoy him. You spiff that little girl up and get her on over here, okay?"

"We'll be there."

"Come as soon as you can," Lou said. "If you're not already here, I'm afraid he won't wait."

"Oh, great. I feel like one of us ought to be carrying a shotgun."

"It may come to that," Lou said. "But right now we make it as painless as possible. That way we keep him off balance."

"Lou—"

"All we're doing here is making it possible for him to come to the right decision," Lou said, apparently anticipating an objection. "Don't worry."

But Corey did worry. She wasn't at all certain it was a good idea to go after a man who was so determinedly resistant. Lou might not have given up on Beltran, but Corey had totally written him off as a lost cause. Even if he was finally willing to see the baby, at this rate he'd come around to fatherhood in time to catch her graduation from college.

"Can you say something to Shorty before you go?" Corey asked. "She's really into telephones this week." She held the receiver to the baby's ear, watching her highly interested expression when she heard Lou's voice. Lou was still talking when Corey took the receiver back.

"'Bye, Lou. We'll be there in a little bit," Corey said as she hung up the phone. "Okay, baby girl, let's go wash the applesauce off your face. We've got to go see the sergeant. What do you want to wear, huh?"

The baby responded in a long string of conversational gibberish, complete with some left-handed finger pointing. She was vocalizing more, Corey was happy to note, but she was still not quite smiling. Sometimes she came so close—when Corey tap-danced around the kitchen or played hide-and-seek with her—but a genuine smile had yet to grace her precious face.

The baby expounded further.

"Really?" Corey said, as if she had understood every word. "Good choice. Too bad your 'cammies' are in the hamper." She smiled to herself, thinking of the green camouflage rompers Lou had brought one day. They would have been very appropriate for today's appointment.

It was past two when Corey finally located a parking space at the Department of Social Services. And it was beginning to rain. Corey wasted no time getting the two of them inside the building. Lou must have been watching for her.

"We finally made it," Corey said when she saw her. "It took forever to find a place to park."

"You didn't happen to see a certain sergeant anywhere on your way in, did you?" Lou asked.

"Don't tell me he's not here."

"No, he's not here," Lou said. "And if that man has backed out, his butt is mine."

Corey sighed. "Well, we can wait. Shorty and I didn't have any big plans for this afternoon. He could still get here. Something could have come up at the last minute. Maybe he's having a hard time finding a parking place, too. Maybe he—"

"There is no excuse for this, Corey—except maybe the outbreak of World War Three—but even then I'd have to think about it," Lou said, hands on her hips. "I am so aggravated!" Suddenly she smiled at the baby. "But I'm not aggravated with you, am I? *What* a pretty baby *girl.* Did I tell you I love that hat? I do. It is *you,* sweet patootie."

The baby reached up to touch the fuzzy brim as if she had followed every word, and both Lou and Corey laughed.

"Well," Lou said. "I need to do some desk work. I guess I'll go do that while we're waiting. You know the drill."

Corey knew. Stay out of the way until sent for. Do *not* initiate contact with the parent on her own. She took the baby to the only empty—and somewhat out-of-the-way—seat in the waiting area and sat to remove the baby's hat and coat. She glanced out the window as she rummaged in her oversize purse for Shorty's favorite kitten book. It was raining hard now, a gray, bleak day that matched Corey's mood. Poor Shorty. It seemed destined to rain whenever she was about to cross paths with her alleged father.

Corey and the baby went through the kitten book. Twice. There was still no sign of Beltran.

Okay, Sergeant. Don't break this little girl's heart.

The only problem was that Corey didn't know which would be the best for the child in the long run—his arrival or his staying away. She kissed the baby on the cheek and gave her the book. At least Shorty was too little to know that there was a very good chance that she had been stood up.

They waited for nearly an hour, until the baby became too cranky to contain in their out-of-the-way location any longer. There were only so many times a budding bibliophile—even one as enthusiastic as this one—could look at assorted cats without wanting to move on to her next literary adventure. Corey hadn't anticipated this kind of delay, and she had only brought the one book. She finally picked the baby up and went looking for Lou. The other woman was still at her desk, and she was not happy.

"Any news?" Corey asked.

"Not one word. I was just coming to tell you to go on home," Lou said. "I'd like to say the game was called on account of rain, but the son-of-a-you-know-what just didn't bother to show up. No phone call. No nothing. And I am surprised—can you believe that? I am really surprised. I mean that man called *me* to set this thing up." She gave a sharp sigh. "You think I'd learn. Well, better luck next time—if there is a next time. And I'm telling you right now he is going to be lucky if I don't break both his feet. It's obvious he doesn't know who he's messing with here."

"Maybe it's for the best," Corey said as she put the baby's coat and hat back on. "Or not," she amended at the look on Lou's face. If Lou Kurian said a man was father material, he was father material—and that was that.

"Oh, get going," Lou said, shooing them away. "And don't get wet. Bye-bye," she said to Shorty, who dutifully bobbed one little hand. "You want me to hold her while you go get the car?"

"No, it's not that far away," Corey said. "We lucked out with the parking space if nothing else."

Corey had only seen Sergeant Beltran one time. If truth be told, she, too, was surprised that he hadn't shown up today. That night, she hadn't been around him long enough to come to any conclusions whatsoever about his character—but she was still surprised.

"I just don't know, Shorty," she said to the baby as she hurried out into the rain toward the car. "All new daddies need to be broken in, I guess. And then there are daddies who need broken feet."

Matt watched the woman and the baby in the white fuzzy hat until they got into a dark green Volvo station wagon. He had arrived at the Department of Social Services shortly after one-thirty, but he didn't go in. He just...sat there, and he had no idea why. He wasn't scared. He would have known if he was scared. He had been in harm's way enough times in several foreign countries. And he knew all about the case of nerves that came with an open jump door at high speed over the drop zone, and death waiting with open arms for something to go wrong on the way to the ground below. Conquering the fear was what it was all about. The shakier the knees, the bigger the high when it was over. But this wasn't anything like that. This was...

He didn't know what it was. All he knew was that when he'd made the dreaded phone call to Lou Kurian, he had fully intended to talk to her about the remote possibility he could have fathered the child and to see the kid. But once he got here, he could only sit in the car. He saw the foster mother and the kid arrive. He saw them leave. And he was still sitting.

The Volvo pulled out into the street; he memorized the license plate number as the woman drove past. He sat there a moment longer, then started the Cor-

vette, waiting for several more cars to go by before
he pulled out of the parking lot and turned in the
same direction. He had every intention of following
her. Discreetly, of course. He didn't know how much
she had been told about him, but he saw no reason
to get her attention if she happened to have been
advised that he was the soldier in question and the
one who hadn't bothered to keep the appointment. If
so, she probably already knew what kind of car he
drove. Everybody on the base seemed to know ''The
Baby Abandoned in Beltran's Red Corvette'' story,
and probably everybody in town, too. It was a miracle it hadn't made the paper or the six-o'clock news.

But right now he just wanted to see where the
woman was going—and hopefully where she lived.
He needed to know more about her. Regardless of
Miss Lou's reassurances, he still wasn't sure this
woman was the best person to be taking care of the
kid. He knew for a fact that when Miss Lou telephoned her, she hadn't wanted to be bothered—not
that he was one to talk. On the other hand, *he* wasn't
supposed to be in the abandoned-baby business.
Maybe the woman had taken her husband's death
really hard. Maybe she was still too messed up to be
looking after a child right now and she knew it. Lou
Kurian wasn't easy to say no to. He could vouch for
that. He certainly hadn't been able to say no and
make it stick. He had only been able to escape her
heavy-handed manipulation by bailing out at the last
minute. When push came to shove, he had won this
round, and he should have been a whole lot happier
about it than he was.

The Volvo went up Bragg Boulevard in the outside lane. He followed for a time, then switched to the inside lane. He could see the baby's car seat in the back, but not the baby. He smiled slightly in spite of himself. That hat was something else.

He lost sight of the car as they rode through an older residential section and the traffic ahead of him abruptly slowed. When it began moving again, he changed lanes to catch up and then drove a little ahead of her. He was glad it was raining. Even if she did know what kind of car he had, she wouldn't be able to tell it was actually him as long as he didn't get too close. He fought down a sudden pang of guilt that she'd had to bring the kid out in this kind of weather for nothing.

He lost her again. Somewhere she must have made a right turn off Bragg Boulevard. It took him a few minutes to find a place to turn around so he could backtrack. He didn't see the Volvo anywhere along the way, but she couldn't have gone far. The only thing left to do was to turn around again and start checking the side streets.

He saw the car parked in the driveway of a small yellow house on the first street he turned down.

Too easy, lady, he thought, more than a little pleased with himself. *Too easy.*

The house sat on the corner of the second block, and he wasn't sure which street it faced. He didn't see the woman or the baby anywhere. He drove by slowly, trying to spot the house number. He realized immediately that the place wasn't nearly as small as he had first thought. It had been built to accommodate a very narrow but deep and downward-sloping lot, and it appeared to have an upstairs. There were two tall pine trees close to the street and several more in the back. Apparently neither the widow nor her late husband had ever taken up the thankless task of trying to coax grass to grow under them. The small yard was a carpet of pine needles. There was a front—or possibly side—porch with just enough room for a swing. Some kind of vine—ivy, he supposed—climbed the latticed porch supports up to the roof.

Not bad, he thought. Kind of 1950s, but certainly adequate for the baby. More than adequate. A hell of a lot better than where she'd come from.

It took two drive-by attempts for him to locate the house number, but the vine was in the way, and he still wasn't sure exactly what it was. He didn't make a third pass, because an old man with a golf umbrella came out of the house across the street and walked down the sidewalk to get his newspaper. He stared pointedly at Matt as he drove past.

Busted, he thought.

There was nothing to do but leave. He didn't want to have to explain to some cop why he was doing a one-man reconnaissance of this particular neighborhood—not when he didn't really know himself.

He nodded to the old man as he turned the corner, hoping to allay any suspicions that he might be stalking the admittedly attractive widow.

Then he took himself to the post library—and the nearest copy of the city directory.

Chapter Five

Corey saw the red Corvette from the kitchen window. Both times. She couldn't see the driver, but she had no doubt whatsoever that it was Beltran.

Doing what, exactly?

And how did he get here?

Corey sighed heavily. It was obvious *how*—he had followed her. The why was much more obscure. Why would he blow off the appointment *he* set up and then go to all the trouble of following her to her house?

She continued to ponder the question as she put Shorty in her high chair. She cut up half a banana for her and poured her some juice. The baby was doing wonderfully with soft finger foods and the training cup, so well that Corey thought she might be older than the doctor had estimated. Pouring the juice out of the cup onto the high chair tray was still very intriguing to the baby, but so was drinking it. Shorty sat and kicked her little legs happily as she ate, offering Corey a squashed piece of banana from time to time.

"Very good!" Corey said when the baby maneuvered the double-handled cup successfully to her mouth and back to the tray. "Look at that big girl drink from a cup!"

Shorty looked at her and very nearly beamed. But she didn't smile.

Corey sat down at the kitchen table and watched the rain beat steadily against the windowpanes, her mind going immediately to the sergeant. Maybe he had been delayed and he really did want to see the baby. Maybe he had arrived at the building just in time to see her and the baby leave, and he'd followed them home, hoping for—

For what?

All he would have had to do was pick up the telephone and call Lou. She would have worked out something. Shorty's future was at stake, and Lou wanted to resolve this situation a lot more than she wanted to do him bodily harm.

But so simple a solution to the problem was apparently unacceptable for someone with a military mind-set. Clearly, Beltran preferred stealth and taking matters into his own hands to anything so reasonable and logical as making a phone call.

Corey glanced around in time to catch Shorty as she was about to road test the effect of gravity on her juice cup.

"Whoa!" she said, nearly fumbling the cup as it

was tossed overboard. She set it out of harm's way and lifted the baby from the high chair, kissing both banana-flavored cheeks soundly. "Okay. This is the plan, see. I let you down. You toddle awhile, and then you nap. Oh, what a good idea!"

The rest of the afternoon went smoothly. It occurred to Corey later that evening, after the baby had been put to bed for the night, that she herself hadn't been especially reasonable and logical. She hadn't telephoned Lou Kurian, either—and she should have. Lou should know that Beltran had kept the appointment, after all—in a manner of speaking. Of course, Corey wasn't absolutely certain it was Beltran who had driven by, except in her woman's-intuition, gut-feeling sort of way that used to drive Jacob to distraction. It could have been...anybody. She supposed.

In a red Corvette.

Who drove by twice.

She stayed alert for the rest of the week, every time she went out and every time she heard a car go by. But she didn't see him again—at least, not driving past the house. On Friday afternoon, she thought she caught a glimpse of a car like his when she went to the grocery store and then again at the bank. But she finally decided she was being silly. She was beginning to feel as if she were trapped in a *Where's Waldo?* book and Beltran was "Waldo." In her more rational moments, she was certain there was no reason to suppose that he might be lurking around every corner. Why would he?

Because he wants to get close to this baby in his own way, she suddenly thought. *He's scared to death he really is her father, and he doesn't know what to do.*

She abruptly smiled to herself.

"It's still working, Jacob," she said aloud. Her sudden flashes of insight had caused more than one disagreement between them.

He had called it jumping to conclusions, and he had often considered her too judgmental. She called it simply paying attention. It had been Jacob's nature to take people at face value, to trust them even when he had good cause not to. Consequently, he had always had to have a house fall on him. It had perturbed him to no end that she would assess the motivation behind some church member's behavior—or misbehavior—based on essentially no concrete information at all...and be right.

"How do you know these things?" he would lament.

"I just do," she'd tell him. It was a bit of a curse, actually, this talent she had for recognizing actual intent. There was hardly ever any justifiable opportunity for her to vent her frustration with other people—not when she could see the reason for their bothersome behavior so clearly.

She finished all her errands, except for the one she had asked old Mr. Rafferty and his wife to sit with Shorty long enough for her to do. She drove to the cemetery. It had been a long time since she'd made a special trip to visit Jacob's grave. Weeks. Months. She had been too busy with the baby, but she went today, bearing both a bouquet of fresh flowers she had bought at the grocery store and her guilt. The sun was shining, the weather perfect for today, at least. A warm breeze blew across her face as she got out of the car.

She had barely noticed the arrival of spring last year, she thought as she walked to Jacob's grave. She realized immediately that someone had planted jonquils there, some thoughtful member of the congregation who meant to give her hope. They were not yet in bloom, and she reached out and lightly touched the headstone, as she always did. It was dry and cold, in spite of the warmth of the sun.

She knelt and began clearing away the debris from the recent rain, stuffing the leaves and broken twigs and bits of paper into the grocery bag with the flowers.

"I'm doing better, Jacob," she whispered as she worked. "You'd like the little baby girl Lou found—in a Corvette, of all places. Can you believe that?"

She suddenly stopped. She had been trying to imagine the sensation of being warmed in one of Jacob's smiles, and she couldn't. He had smiled all the time. It was one of the first things she'd noticed about him—his beautiful smile. She closed her eyes for a moment. Why couldn't she remember?

She gave a wavering sigh. There was nothing. She could feel the sun on her face, and the breeze. She could feel the cold, damp ground against her knees. But she couldn't feel Jacob. He wasn't here. It had never been like this before. Even when her grief had been at its most profound, she had been able to talk to him, and believe that he heard her. It had been a real comfort to her—her only comfort, actually—telling him everything, anything. She hadn't been able to draw any kind of strength from Jacob's congregation or from her family. Only from him.

But there was no comfort now. In the time she had stayed away, his grave, his headstone, had become like all the others—a lifeless, joyless symbol of someone who had once been. She suddenly bowed her head in a concentrated effort to fight down the intense loneliness that threatened to overwhelm her. She had managed to keep it at bay for all this time, for all the weeks she had been taking care of Beltran's little girl, and now she had run right smack into it, as strong as ever, as implacable as ever.

She made a small sound at the realization.

Jacob is really gone.

She didn't cry. She had no tears left anymore. It wasn't sorrow that she felt. It was more akin to physical pain.

She had no idea how long she stayed like that. Eventually, she took the flowers from the grocery bag and unwrapped them, placing them one by one into the heavy vase at the foot of the headstone. She took the time to carefully arrange the spring flowers—daisies and sweet Williams, lilies and baby's breath—the kind that he had always given her.

But when she had finished, she barely looked at her handiwork. She stood and walked quickly away, her mind still in turmoil.

Is this how it's going to be? I can't hear his voice anymore. I can't see his face. Am I going to lose everything of him?

Oh, Jacob.

She hardly remembered the drive home. And when she parked the car in the drive, she was surprised to find she had been crying, after all. She wiped furtively at her eyes. She could see Carla Rafferty holding the baby up at the window. so they both could officially greet her.

Corey took a deep breath and got out, waving to Shorty before she began to unload the groceries from the back of the station wagon. Her head ached. She was emotionally exhausted, and for once she didn't look up at the sound of a passing car.

Only the car didn't pass. It stopped dead in the middle of the street. She jumped violently and looked around when the driver laid on the horn. Beltran was getting out on the driver's side.

"You want to tell me what the hell is wrong with you?" he asked. The quiet tone of his voice completely belied the expression on his face.

Matt thought for a brief moment that she was completely out of it, because she looked at him so blankly. But then she took a deep breath and went back to unloading the groceries. If she recognized him from the night they'd met, she didn't show it. He wasn't in uniform, and it was very possible that she didn't.

"Are you sick?" he persisted. "Or drunk?"

That got her attention.

"What are you talking about?" she said.

He stepped back and slammed the car door. "You drove through a stoplight back there, lady. You've been driving crazy all the way up the boulevard."

She frowned and, surprisingly, didn't deny it. She went back to the groceries.

"You could have killed somebody."

She glanced at him and took out another grocery bag. He thought she was about to cry.

"Look," he said. "Are you...okay? I didn't mean to scare you or anything. I just thought you—"

"You thought I had the baby in the car," she interrupted. "I didn't. Not that that matters. I could have. I—" She took a deep breath. "I really am very careful where she is concerned, but you were...right to call me on it, Sergeant."

So, he thought, *she does remember me.*

He came closer. He wasn't about to be put off that easily. He wanted to see for himself, up close and personal, if she was all right or not.

They stared at each other, and he recognized the expression on her face immediately. It was that quick-hide-your-wives-and-daughters one some people got every time they ran into a military man.

"I am *not* under the influence," she said finally.

He nodded, accepting her assertion because he could see now that she was telling the truth. "So where is she?" he asked. "The baby."

"Inside," she said. "With a sitter. Two sitters actually. If you want to see her, you had better move your car."

He stayed where he was, not sure he'd heard right.

"Isn't that against some rule?" he asked. "You letting me see her?"

"Actually, I'm not sure. But you're here, and you're anxious about her. So you might as well come in and see how she is for yourself."

"I'm not—" *Anxious,* he was about to say. But that wasn't the truth. He was anxious, damn it. His rampant anxiety had been the whole point of his following her back here in the first place. When he saw her run that red light, he simply hadn't been able to let it go.

"Okay," he said, getting back into the car. He pulled forward and parked at the curb.

When he got out, she had already gone into the house with the groceries, carrying all the bags herself. He half expected her to bolt the door once she cleared the porch, and call the police.

But she didn't. She handed the grocery bags to an elderly man who stood just inside the screen door and then immediately came back outside again. Matt didn't waste any time getting to the porch steps, because he didn't want to give her—or himself—the opportunity to think about the advisability of what they were doing. As far as he was concerned, the jump door was open and they were over the drop. There was no backing out now.

"Corey Madsen," she said, extending her hand as he stepped up on the porch.

Yes, I know, he almost said, then decided against it. He didn't want her to think he was some kind of crazed stalker, even if finding out who she was hadn't been all that difficult. He had simply looked up the address and then the name in the city directory. Her late husband was Jacob Madsen. She had been identified in parentheses as "Corey D., tcher." He wondered idly if she was teaching anything these days. He thought not, unless the two elderly sitters— who were standing behind her and obviously ready to take a broom to him if the situation warranted it— looked after the kid while she worked.

The Madsen woman was still holding out her

hand, and he abruptly shook it. Her grasp was firm, but her fingers were cold in his. He saw, now that he was closer, that she had been crying, and he suspected it had resulted in her erratic driving. Her eyes were all puffy and red. When she realized he was staring at her, she looked away.

"I...appreciate this," he said.

"You hope," she countered, voicing his misgivings so accurately that he almost let himself smile.

"Come inside," she said. "This is Mr. and Mrs. Rafferty, my neighbors from across the street. This is...I'm sorry, I don't know your first name."

"Matt," he said. "Mateo, actually."

The old guy with the golf umbrella, he thought, nodding to them both. *Busted again. Great.*

"Matt Beltran," Corey said. "He's a sergeant—"

"Staff sergeant," he corrected. He wanted to keep the record straight. And he wanted the old man to know he wasn't obscuring his identity in any way, regardless of the first impression.

"He's a jump master out at the base," Corey said.

Right, Matt thought, looking at all their wary faces. *And a beer-drinking scumbag who likes to nail exotic dancers and then not remember.*

"And this is...well, I really can't tell you who this is, Sergeant," Corey said, gesturing to the baby. "We call her Shorty."

"'Shorty'?" he said, staring at the baby girl who watched him so gravely from the safety of Mrs. Rafferty's arms.

What the hell kind of name is Shorty? he thought.

"That's some of Buck's crazy doing," Mrs. Rafferty said as if he had spoken aloud. "You should have heard what he called *our* kids. The one that was always losing his diaper? He called him Moon Pie—''

''Well, what else would you call him, Mother?'' Buck said, grinning at the baby.

The baby waved one hand at him, and Mrs. Rafferty rolled her eyes.

''And it wasn't just our young-uns,'' she said. ''Right to this day, there is a fifty-year-old man—a big shot, let me tell you—running around this town *still* being called Dingle. That was Buck's doing, too—and don't you ask *why* he called him that.''

Matt tried to stand firm, tried to follow the lively and decidedly down-home conversation. But the truth was, it had been a long time since he had felt this ill at ease. The widow had been crying—and might start again, for all he knew. The neighbors were expecting him to do something uncouth. And the baby—

He kept looking at the baby. She was a pretty little kid. Hell, she was beautiful. Really beautiful. The picture didn't do her justice. She had dark eyes—like his—and she returned his gaze for a moment, then abruptly reached for Corey, who smiled and took her.

''Have you been a good girl?'' Corey asked. ''Yes?''

''Good as gold,'' the old man said.

''I knew it,'' Corey said, kissing the baby's cheek. ''You're always a good girl. Are you a hungry baby?''

''She probably could eat a little something,'' Mrs. Rafferty said. ''She's slept about the whole time you were gone.''

"Anything but green beans, right?" Corey teased. The baby hid her face in Corey's shoulder. "Ah. Shy baby, too." She rubbed her gently on her back.

"Corey, do you want us to stay?" Rafferty asked pointedly, glancing in Matt's direction.

"If you would, Buck. The sergeant and Shorty and I are going out to the kitchen. We won't be long. This way, Sergeant Beltran," she said.

He followed. They might be on her turf, but he had no intention of letting her call all the shots. Unfortunately, Corey Madsen wasn't the least bit interested in giving him the opportunity to demonstrate his ability to take charge of the situation.

"Is this baby yours or not?" she asked immediately and without prelude.

He looked at her steadily over the baby's head. "I...don't know."

"Are you going to try to find out? Or does that depend on whether or not she passes inspection."

"Is that why you think I want to see her? So I can decide if she's worth going to the trouble?"

"Isn't it?"

"Look, you and Miss Lou started this whole deal with the picture and the progress report."

"And you didn't keep the appointment *you* made. Of course, she's only a daughter, and not a son. I'm sure—for some men—that must be an important consideration."

Her remark really annoyed him, but he didn't show it. He hoped. There was a shriek and then boisterous laughter from the Raffertys in the other room, and he turned to look in that direction.

"Are they always like that?" he asked, because the giggling immediately escalated.

"Always," she said.

"Newlyweds?"

"Hardly. They had their fifty-fifth anniversary last year. Okay!" she called loudly to the rowdy couple in the other room. "Don't make me come in there!"

The giggling started all over again. The combination of marriage and laughter was a completely foreign concept to him. He had grown up in a children's home staffed by priests and nuns. He didn't know anything about marriage. And the ones he'd had to deal with on the base, the ones his people were forever living to regret, didn't give rise to anything even remotely resembling mirth—for them or him.

"Could I hold her?" he asked abruptly. He was comfortable around children. At Holy Angels he had been the big brother and father figure for more kids than he could count. To tell the truth, he had kind of liked the adoration. It hadn't taken much effort on his part to get it. A kind word to a little kid, maybe a threat or two to a school yard bully, and he had been able to make a friend for life.

The widow looked at him doubtfully. "If she'll come to you," she said finally.

"Put her down—she's walking now, isn't she?"

"Yes, but—"

"I'm not going to upset her. I'm just going to sit here on the floor—and she can walk around and look at me. Okay?"

She hesitated before she answered. "Okay...but you probably ought to be doing something interesting. Here," she said, handing him a bag of groceries. "This is the one with the meat sticks."

"Meat sticks," he said, looking into the bag and expecting to see the beef jerky sold at the cash register in the convenience stores. But these particular ones were in a glass baby-food-type jar.

"Her absolute personal favorite."

"So she's not much of a vegetarian," he said, sitting cross-legged on the floor.

"If she had a few more teeth, you could hire a limo and take her to the Rose Garden and buy her a steak."

He tried not to smile. The woman had a sense of humor—even if her eyes were red from crying. But it was important for him to remain detached and in control. It was also important not to scare the kid. And it was absolutely imperative that he stay focused. Unfortunately, sitting on the floor the way he was, he had a nice view of the Madsen legs.

A very nice view.

He couldn't help but see them; the woman wore a dress. And she had an excellent reason to wear dresses.

He had to firmly remind himself that he was *not* here for the scenery, impressive and thought-provoking though it might be. He was here to find out about the kid. And then he could make his plans accordingly.

Shorty wanted down, and Corey put her on the floor. The baby wobbled for a moment until she got her balance, then she stood looking at Matt as he conspicuously rummaged in the bag Corey had handed him.

"Hey, Shorty," he whispered. "What's in here? What could it be?"

The baby looked up at Corey and made a definite but completely incomprehensible verbal inquiry, more or less pointing at him as she asked.

"Go ahead," Corey said. "It's okay."

"You speak the language fluently, I see," he said, keeping his eyes on the baby instead of the Madsen legs.

"Actually, I'm hopeless," she said. "But I know whatever she wants has to do with you and the grocery bag—and I recognize the hand gestures. They're the same as when she worried about whether or not I'm about to turn on the vacuum cleaner."

"So is she smiling yet?" he asked, glancing up in time to see the widow's surprise that he was so well informed. "Miss Lou told me she didn't smile," he said, and whether he wanted to or not, he sounded as if he thought it was all Corey Madsen's fault.

And maybe he did want to. She hadn't exactly been thrilled to take the kid—and kids picked up on things like that.

"She almost smiles every now and then—when she forgets she doesn't want to. Sort of like you," Corey said. She turned away and began putting cans into the kitchen cabinet.

Way to go, Widow Madsen, he thought. *Don't let the bad old sergeant push you around.*

The baby toddled closer.

"Hey, Shorty, what's in here, huh?" he asked her, holding the bag out to her. She came immediately and looked in, struggling to get a can of fruit cocktail out.

"Take it to Corey," he said. "She really needs it." And regardless of the fact that he was used to having his orders immediately carried out, he was amazed that the baby turned to do just that. "Outstanding!" he said.

"Oh, thank you," Corey said elaborately when Shorty more or less presented the can. "Where does it go? Right here? Okay. Right *here*."

Corey put the can on the shelf, and Shorty immediately returned for another dip into the bag.

"Another one?" Corey said of the next delivery. "Oh, boy! Another one!"

"Tat-too," Shorty said.

"Thank you," Corey echoed, her eyes meeting his. He could see the question in them. He could see how hard she was working at trying to decide what he was really up to. He didn't know himself exactly. He only knew that he had questions of his own, questions like the one he'd started out with.

What the hell is wrong with you?

He was still irked by her recklessness. People—not to mention a government agency—depended on her. This baby depended on her. She had no business driving the way she had, whether the kid was in the car or not.

And looking at her now, he thought he knew the reason. She was still grieving. He could look into her sad eyes and tell that. She must have been having a bad day, and had to get away by herself for a while. That was admirable, he supposed—if she knew she was going to bawl over her dead husband and didn't want the kid to see her. Crying in the dark or crying in a car—the same difference when you got right down to it, except that the latter was a lot more dangerous.

The baby was growing more accustomed to him. She held on to his arm to look into the grocery bag for the next item, "talking" about the project at length as she dragged out another can.

"Roger that," he said, as if he understood. "Too easy. Right? *Too* easy."

He waited until she'd removed all the cans before he let her see the meat sticks. Corey had been absolutely correct. Meat sticks were this kid's all-time personal favorite. She grabbed the jar and clutched it to her chest, bobbing up and down with a squeal of delight.

"See?" Corey said.

"Yeah, I see. I wonder if the Pentagon knows about these things. They may be better than what we get in the field. You are going to crack open the jar?" he asked as he got to his feet. The kid hung on to the meat sticks for dear life in case he had designs on them, and clutched the leg of his jeans with her other hand.

"Of course," she said, and she would have picked the baby up herself if he hadn't beaten her to it.

"She needs her hands washed—"

"I'll do it," he said. "If that's okay."

They looked at each other. She obviously had her doubts about that. Really big ones.

But for whatever reason, she abruptly gave in. "The bathroom is down the hall on the left," she said. "You'll need to—"

"I can do it," he interrupted. "Really. I know a lot about kids. Don't worry."

He waited for further protest, but she didn't say anything else. He took the baby to the bathroom, navigating between the Raffertys to get there.

"You got your work cut out for you, son," Buck said, and Matt actually let himself smile.

"Hoo-ah," he said to agree.

The hand-washing turned out to be a little more complicated than he'd anticipated, but he managed. When he returned, the Raffertys and the widow had their heads together. He pretended not to notice.

"Okay, Short Stuff. Get ready for inspection," he said. "Check it out, Mrs. Madsen. Clean hands *and* clean meat stick jar—you didn't think she was going to let go of it, did you?"

Corey laughed. "No, I didn't. Do you want to put her in the high chair?"

He did, but he needed some help with that, mostly because Shorty had him by the neck of his T-shirt and wasn't the least bit inclined to let him or the meat sticks go. Eventually, he got her situated and the jar opened. And he noticed that the Raffertys were still on guard duty, but no longer relegated to the other room.

"Buck and I will feed her, Matt," Mrs. Rafferty said to him. "You may want to talk to Corey."

Did he?

He suddenly realized that it didn't matter whether he did or not. The plan was for him to be on his way, and the Widow Madsen was waiting to show him how it was done.

He stood for a moment, watching as the Raffertys got Shorty all involved in chowing down, then he followed the widow out onto the porch.

"You need to call Lou," she said. She walked to the edge and looked down at the ground.

"I need to know why you've still got the kid," he countered.

She looked at him. "I don't know what you mean."

"You only agreed to take her for a day or two, until Miss Lou could find somebody else, isn't that right?"

"Yes."

"Well, I want to know why she's still here if you don't want her. She shouldn't be in a place where she's not wanted—"

"You are very mistaken about that, Sergeant. I do want her—that's *why* she's still here. I absolutely love that little girl. So do the Raffertys. She has that effect on people. You're going to have to be very careful if you're planning on seeing her again."

He didn't say anything.

"Are you planning on seeing her again?" she asked pointedly.

"I want to do whatever is best for her," he said truthfully.

"You think she is yours then."

"I told you before. I don't know. I honest-to-God do not know. Rita—her mother—"

He stopped, and he actually reached into his pocket for a cigarette, when he hadn't smoked for nearly a year. The widow moved to the swing and sat down. The denim dress that didn't quite come to her knees rode up.

"I guess that shocks you—the fact that I can't remember," he said abruptly.

"No. It doesn't shock me," she said. "I'm sure there were…circumstances."

"Circumstances? Yeah, I guess you could call it that. I went to one of the clubs on the Boulevard. I had too much to drink. It's not something I do on a regular basis, but that time I—" He glanced at her. Damned if he was going to make excuses, regardless of the huge opening she had given him. She wasn't looking at him, but she was still listening.

He could hear the Raffertys in the kitchen, laughing again.

"This guy I knew—another sergeant," he went on. "We were at Fort Benning together—airborne school. He was on the tarmac the day they had the midair collision out at Pope. He was checking out the group that was getting ready to go up for a training jump. I was supposed to do it, but I…"

He frowned. He didn't want to talk about this. Why was he talking about this?

"He took your place as jump master?" she asked quietly.

"I couldn't go up. I had this ear thing. I was grounded and, yeah, he took my place."

"He was killed?"

"He died…later. He hung on for as long as he could—weeks—but then he died. The Corvette was his. The son of a bitch left it to me. I don't know if it was to show me he didn't have any hard feelings or if he wanted to make sure I'd remember who…took it for me. What I was supposed to get, he took. Either way, I have to keep the car, because I—" He exhaled sharply and looked out across the yard, focusing on what he could see and not on what he could remember.

Pine needles. Sand. A bush with yellow flowers.

"Anyway," he said abruptly, looking back at her. "The night he died, I got drunk. I remember Rita Warren being there. She worked at the club—if you can call what she does work. But I don't remember what happened—what I did. If the kid *is* mine, she never said—" He stopped again. This was getting way out of hand. "Sorry. I don't know why I'm telling you this. The details don't matter. I can't change anything. It's done, and that's the whole sad story."

"Except for what happens now."

"I guess I'll have to do what you said. I'll have to talk to Lou Kurian and get with the program— whatever the program is."

"Well, I wouldn't do it in person."

"Why not?"

"Because she's planning on breaking both your feet."

He laughed, caught off guard again by her surprising sense of humor. "That sounds like Miss Lou," he said. "She could probably do it, too."

The widow smiled, but then the smile faded.

"I can't let you see the baby again unless you make some kind of arrangement with Lou."

"Understood," he said. He made a point of looking into her eyes simply because he knew it made her uncomfortable. She tried to hold his gaze and couldn't.

He heard the telephone ring somewhere in the house, and then Mrs. Rafferty came to the door.

"Corey, come here, honey," she said, calling her over, but he could still hear their conversation.

"There's somebody on the phone," Mrs. Rafferty whispered, though her whispers sounded louder than most people talked.

"Who?" Corey said in a normal voice.

"Honey, she asked for Reverend Madsen. She didn't know one thing about Jacob dying. I think maybe she's one of them young-uns from Jacob's support group—one of them kids that was fighting drugs and trying to find out what to do with themselves and everything. Could you come talk to her? She's really upset, and I just don't know what to tell her."

"All right," Corey said to her. "I'll be right back," she called to Matt.

He stood there. Frowning.

Reverend Madsen.

Reverend.

Corey Madsen's late husband was a preacher.

Well, that's just great, he thought. So much for city directories. Too bad he hadn't noticed that little detail *before* he made a fool of himself, telling her that he had been so drunk he didn't know whether or not he had hooked up with a woman who went topless and made sexual overtures to a brass pole for a living.

Ah, damn!

Corey Madsen had been a preacher's wife. What would she know about people like Rita—and him? She had said she wasn't shocked. Hell, it was a wonder she didn't have to be resuscitated.

He sighed heavily. At least he'd gotten a chance

to see the kid on neutral ground. He probably wouldn't get another one—at least not here. He went to the door and lightly knocked. Mrs. Rafferty came immediately. She had the baby in her arms.

"Would you tell Corey—Mrs. Madsen—I had to go?" he asked. "And Shorty—" he began, looking at the baby. She immediately leaned out and pressed one little hand against the screen door. He touched it briefly with his fingers. He could almost, but not quite, feel her warmth through the wire mesh. "Well, I guess she's too little to understand. Maybe I—" He stopped. He wasn't ready to make any promises.

Mrs. Rafferty stood looking at him. She reminded him of one of the sisters at the children's home, the one who always knew exactly what he was up to and who always forgave him for it.

"You come back and see us, Matt," she said. "We'll be here."

Chapter Six

"What's wrong?" Beltran asked.

"Nothing," Corey said, but still she made no move to unlock the screen door. Her eyes were on the car that was driving slowly past, the one filled with several women from the church, who were obviously startled to see a soldier standing on her front porch.

Standing, she wanted to point out to them. Not coming inside the house.

It had never occurred to Corey that, to some people, these newly approved visitations from Shorty's alleged father would look like…*something.*

"I talked to Miss Lou," he said, clearly puzzled by her behavior.

She glanced at him. Even if the members hadn't seen him—which they had—Beltran's hardly inconspicuous car was parked at the curb. The members would know that *nobody* in a red Corvette could be visiting Corey Madsen on church business. Nobody in the congregation had a car like that. It was likely that nobody in the congregation even *knew* anybody with a car like that. She was "poor Corey" to all of Jacob's flock, and a red Corvette in front of her house could only mean that she was in desperate need of some kind of major intervention on their part.

"I thought you were expecting me," he said.

Oh, the heck with this, Corey suddenly thought. There was absolutely nothing wrong with his being here; she knew that. This was official Department of Social Services business. She didn't owe anyone any explanations.

"Oh, I was expecting you," she said. "Just not on the right day at the right time." She watched an array of emotions flit across his face, and she tried not to smile. He definitely had a censored response to that remark, but he changed his mind about saying it. Several times.

"You know what, Mrs. Madsen?" he said finally. "At first you seem like such a nice, polite little person—but you have got a mouth on you."

This time she did smile, and she unlocked the door to let him in. "I know," she said, pushing the screen open. "I'm ashamed of it, but there you are."

"So where's Shorty?" he asked, trying to maintain his usual no-nonsense air.

"Waking up from her nap, I think. You can go check, if you want. Second door on the left down the hall."

"It's okay to get her if she's awake?"

"If she's not scared of you."

"We've met before," he reminded her.

"She might not recognize you. You're wearing fatigues today. You weren't the last time."

"Given her mother's line of work, I expect she's used to seeing guys in fatigues. Anyway, we'll work it out," he assured her. He went down the hall, and he came back again almost immediately.

"Still pushing the z's," he said from the kitchen doorway. He came in and sat at the kitchen table, and he seemed to have no compunction whatsoever about whether or not he would be welcome.

"Coffee?" Corey said after a moment. He wasn't in the way, but he might as well have been. She had noticed the other afternoon how crowded a room suddenly became with him in it—with that intimidating mix of lean, mean physical presence and in-your-face attitude.

"If it's not against some rule—what?" he asked, apparently at the expression on her face. "You don't think I follow rules?"

"I suppose you have to, being in the military." She got down a cup and poured him some coffee.

"Only if you want to stay. Thanks," he said, taking the cup.

"And you want to?"

"Yeah."

"Why?"

"You mean besides the poker and the whiskey and the wild women?"

"Yes," she said evenly, fully aware that he was trying to annoy her with his assessment of her civilian biases.

"I couldn't say. Must be something, though."

"What is it you do, anyway? Besides order people to jump out of planes, I mean."

"I don't order them. They're very happy to oblige."

"What if somebody decides not to oblige?" she said.

"I give them a well-aimed boot out the jump door."

She looked at him, trying to decide if he was stretching the truth or not.

Not, she decided. She had no problem imagining him keeping the line moving—by whatever means necessary.

"What else do you do?" she asked.

"This and that. Whatever they tell me mostly," he said. "Good coffee," he added.

"Thank you. So where are you from?" she asked next, determined now to get some kind of information out of him.

"From?"

"It's not a trick question, Beltran. Where were you born? Where did you grow up? Where did you go to school?"

"A place you never heard of," he said.

"In what state?" she persisted.

He smiled slightly. "Do you grill everybody like this?"

"Only the people who come to see Shorty," she said.

"So where were *you* born? Where did you grow up? Where did you go to school?"

"I asked first."

"East Texas," he said.

"And that is the answer to?"

"All three questions."

"Tell me about East Texas."

"You've never been there?"

"I've never been anywhere. Tell me about it."

"It's hot and humid and it's got bayous."

"Like Louisiana?"

"Just like Louisiana."

"What about Cajun food?"

"That, too. And mosquitoes."

"Did you like it there?"

He didn't answer.

"Did you—"

"I'm thinking!" he said, and she laughed.

She waited, looking at him expectantly.

"I must not have," he said finally. "I left, and I've never been back."

"Why not?"

"Nothing to go back to."

"No family?"

"Not that I know of."

She didn't say anything. She pulled out a chair and sat at the table.

"Go ahead and say it," he said.

"Say what?"

"What everybody says when I tell them I don't have any family. 'Too bad' or 'I'm sorry.'"

"Well, I would have to know more about your situation before I could say that," she said. "I don't know one way or the other. It may not be bad at all. It may be for the best."

"There you go," he agreed, taking another sip of the coffee he'd pronounced "good."

"And maybe you've got family right here," she said.

He looked at her sharply, but he made no comment.

"So what did you like about Texas?" she asked after a moment.

"East Texas," he said.

"There's a difference?"

"Big one," he assured her.

"I'm glad to know that. So what did you like about *East* Texas?"

"Are you always this—" He held up one hand, as though grasping for the word.

"Nosy," she said for him. "The word you're looking for is *nosy*. I told you I was. I like to be informed."

"One of the original inquiring minds."

"Something like that. Only I have to ask. I can't be seen buying supermarket tabloids."

He smiled. "No, that wouldn't do."

"People would talk."

"I'll just bet."

She looked at him, then immediately glanced away. It had been a long time since she had participated in this kind of male-female banter. She would have thought that she no longer knew how, and she was a little ashamed of herself that she remembered so well. Of course, that wasn't the point. The point was that she shouldn't be remembering at all, much less taking part. She was, by no stretch of the imagination, a "merry widow." She hardly knew this man. And given her position as foster parent and the current unresolved situation with his probable child, he wasn't someone with whom she should allow any kind of familiarity whatsoever.

She glanced at Beltran again, and he was waiting for her to do just that. He had the most disconcerting habit of staring directly at her when he was speaking to her—and when he wasn't. She supposed it was something he had perfected in the military, a way of knowing who was going to need that boot out the jump door, or just general intimidating. She wished she had poured herself some coffee. She needed something to do with her hands.

"It's your turn," he advised her.

She almost sighed. She needed a safe topic of conversation. It was clear that he wasn't going to tell her anything about himself if he could help it and, barring East Texas, there didn't seem to be any other neutral subjects. She didn't want to bring up Rita Warren. Or the Balkans. Or his friend who had died. And the current status of his paternity testing, if any, hardly seemed proper.

She immediately imagined the church women at the door.

What are you doing, Corey?

Oh, nothing. Just talking to the sergeant here about his paternity test.

And it really was none of her business. Her sole responsibility was to take care of the baby, and that responsibility was finite. The day would come when her services were no longer needed, regardless of the outcome of his test.

But she didn't want to think about that. She

glanced in the direction of the hall, thinking—hoping—she had heard Shorty awaken.

There was nothing.

"I grew up in a children's home," he volunteered when she looked back at him.

She didn't quite know what to say. She only knew that he was waiting for her to say it.

"Was it a good place to be?" she asked finally.

"I don't know. I don't have anything to compare it to. We had to work hard—chores and all that."

"They didn't beat you or anything?"

Once again, he gave her the barest of smiles. "Only when I needed it."

"I'm sorry," she said, finally giving the token response he'd expected earlier.

"Don't be. The rules were very definite. And they were fair. I knew what they were and I knew the consequences. My choice, my pain."

"Is that what they told you?"

"No, that's the truth."

"Was it a big place—the home?"

"Actually, it was a working farm. It was in the middle of nowhere. No real towns close by, just a kind of country store and gas station at a crossroad a few miles away. The boys' dormitory was on one side of this little secondary road and the girls' was on the other. They were big two-story brick buildings with screened-in front porches on both stories, and a lot of shade trees in the front. The boys used to get to sleep on their second-story porch in the summertime. You think it gets hot here. It's nothing like it is in East Texas. We'd hang mosquito netting on this long rope from one end of the porch to the other and we'd sleep under it. We always got the giggles, and Father Andrew would have to come out and settle us down. Or course, priests are pretty funny-looking when you wake them up like that—and that would set us off again, and he'd really get aggravated. So then we'd count stars—see who could get the most.''

"How did you know who won?" she asked, trying to imagine him as a giggling, mischievous little boy.

"It didn't matter. Nobody could stay awake long enough to count very many anyway."

"You were close—you and the other children who lived there?"

"Let's just say nobody messed with us—at least not more than once."

"What happened if somebody did?"

"We got together and kicked butt."

"And Father Andrew didn't mind?"

"Officially, he didn't know. But, no, I don't think he did mind—as long as it was righteous butt-kicking. He wanted us to be a family, and families look out for each other."

"You lived there a long time?"

"From the time I was six until I joined the army when I was eighteen. The army's not a whole lot different. It's full of orphans, too, only most of them have parents."

"What happened to your parents?"

"They were killed in a car wreck not too far from Holy Angels. Thanks to Father Andrew, I eventually went there to live. I really can't remember very much about the accident or very much about my mother and father. Somebody said I had a concussion or something."

"You didn't have any other relatives?"

"No. Father Andrew looked, but if there were any, he couldn't find them. But I think he—"

Shorty was awake and fretting now. He didn't ask Corey's permission, but got up and went, and this time he stayed in the baby's room. She could hear him talking to the baby, and there was an abrupt cessation in the crying. Shorty must not have been put off by his wearing camouflage after all. Perhaps she was used to it, or perhaps she was used to Beltran.

Corey frowned. Somehow she would rather think that his relationship with Rita Warren was nothing more than a one-night stand rather than consider the very real possibility that he might have been a "regular."

After a moment she went to Shorty's room to see if he or the baby needed anything. He was sitting on the floor, turning the pages of the assortment of books Shorty kept bringing him.

"Is my time up?" he asked.

"No. I just came to see if she was hungry. She usually eats when she gets up."

"Let me guess. Meat sticks."

Corey smiled. "No. After the nap, it's fruit and a cookie. Maybe a little juice or milk."

"Outstanding!" he said to Shorty, lifting her high in the air. Incredibly, she laughed. Out loud.

Infinitely pleased with himself, Beltran looked at Corey and gave her a wink. "There you go," he said.

Too easy!

It was scary how easy it was. To show up twice a

week to see the kid. And to look forward to it. He
even stayed for supper once—homemade potato
soup, with shredded cheese and some kind of finely
chopped, peppery, vinegary onions on top. And
homemade bread.

Outstanding.

He would have wrestled Corey to the floor for that
meal if she hadn't invited him. Of course, he had
reached the point where he would have wrestled her
to the floor for no reason whatsoever. God, she
smelled good and she looked good. All the time.

And he had been talking too much. Telling her
things he had never told anybody. It wasn't as if he
was volunteering the information exactly. The
woman asked him a million questions. She had this
way of looking at him when she did it that somehow
made him *not* resent the fact that she did indeed like
to be "informed." And the next thing he knew he
was shooting off his mouth about anything and everything. The crazy part was that he actually *liked*
talking to her. She didn't let him push her around,
either, and he liked that, too.

And Shorty. Sweet, *laughing* little Shorty.

Corey had been right to warn him about the effect
this baby girl had on people. He was getting so used
to her. He didn't go anywhere these days without her
in mind—the supermarket, the bookstore, the bakery.
He was always looking for something to buy her.
Nothing big. He knew Corey and Miss Lou well
enough to know that the eyebrows would go up if he
did anything too extravagant. Just little things. A kitten book here, a cupcake there—and he'd had to take
a *whole* lot of ragging in the checkout line over that

kitten book. He even bought disposable diapers now and then to help out. Foster parenting, he had learned from Miss Lou, did *not* bring in the big bucks.

He was happier than he had ever been in his life, and a thousand warning bells were going off inside his head all the time. It was too good to be true. It wasn't going to last. He knew that. He should have his head examined for letting himself get this involved in something that would only bring him grief in the long run. If the kid wasn't his, then what? If she was, then what? And what if Rita showed up again and wanted her? He'd never have a minute's peace if he thought Shorty was back in that kind of life. Yet he knew perfectly well that *he* couldn't make any kind of home for her. He had no relatives, no mother or grandmother or aunt to send for to come look after her while he did what he had to do on the post or in Italy or Haiti or the Balkans or the Middle East or wherever the hell else the lid blew off. And he couldn't leave the military. It was his life. It was who and what he was.

He swore under his breath. He was knee-deep in exactly the kind of situation he had always been determined to avoid. Strung up. Worried. All the time.

"Yo! Beltran!" somebody said, and he looked around.

Burke. He'd only been back on the post a few days and was still annoyed that Matt's Balkan time had been cut short without his having been consulted. And the fact that he hadn't been able to find out *why* Matt had come back early only irked him more.

"What's this I'm hearing about you, Matt?" he said.

Matt ignored him.

"Let me see," he persisted, coming closer and staring into Matt's face. "Well, damn if you don't. I can see it," he said, pointing. "You *have* got a ring in your nose. I heard it, but I didn't believe it—out buying diapers, going to see this *fine* widow woman all the time—"

The phone rang and Matt pointedly answered it.

"So are you parking your jump boots under the widow's bed yet?" Burke said as soon as he hung up. "Oh, what the hell am I thinking! This is Beltran we're talking about here. Of *course* he's getting it—"

"What do you want, Burke?" he said, determined not to let the bastard provoke him. If he did, if he gave even an inkling of how close he was to losing his temper, Burke would make his life hell—particularly if the higher-ups were stupid enough to give Burke the promotion he was up for.

"It's not what *I* want, son. It's what the *captain* wants. He says he's short a sergeant, and you, my boy, have just volunteered to take up the slack, starting, oh, twenty minutes ago. If it's all right with the widow, of course. Now, if you think she'll be too lonesome, I'll be glad to run over there and see what I can do. I hear widows are worth the trouble. They really appreciate a man's doing what he can—"

Matt pushed past him without comment. He was supposed to go see the baby—and Corey—this afternoon. Who knew how long this little task of the captain's would take—a long time if Burke had had anything to do with setting it up. And how the man had found out as much as he had about his personal business was beyond him. It was a special talent Burke had—finding out things he could use to provoke his victims into doing something rash. And Matt had been on Burke's hit list for a *long* time.

"You have fun now, you hear?" Burke called after him to get in one last dig.

Son of a bitch, he thought. He'd been all over the world, and every place he'd ever been had at least one Burke in it. He knew what old Father Andrew would say about Burke and his kind. They served a purpose. They were the thorns of the world, without whom other men would never be spurred to rise above their own base natures.

But not this time. Matt had been trying to fight off being overtaken by his lesser self for days. He had that feeling again, the one that had kept him sitting in the car at the Department of Social Services. Not fear. Panic. He realized suddenly how much he needed an excuse to back off from this fatherhood thing. And old Burke had just given it to him. It had fallen—guilt-free—right into his lap; a chance to see how much being a parent really mattered to him, a chance to go back to the way things were, a chance to come to his senses.

He looked over his shoulder at Burke and smiled.

"He didn't show *again?*" Lou asked.

"No," Corey said. "He didn't."

"How many visits has he missed?"

"Four."

"You haven't heard from him?"

"Not a word."

"You think he had to go do the paratrooper thing someplace?"

"How would *I* know?" Corey said more peevishly than she intended, and Lou held up both hands.

"Take it easy, will you? I'm not the jerk here."

Corey frowned. "Sorry. I'm just so…" She sighed heavily.

"I know the feeling, honey. Well, I can check and see if he's still here on the base."

"And if he is?"

"Well, then I go see him and I eloquently express my assessment of his recent behavior *and* his family tree as loudly and in front of as many witnesses as I possibly can."

"I'd rather you broke something," Corey said.

Lou laughed. "Is Shorty all right?"

"Yes, I think so. She looks for him, but hopefully she's still too young to know what's going on. And I think she's kind of used to people disappearing."

"Maybe he's got a good explanation," Lou suggested.

"No, he doesn't. The novelty wore off, that's all. Anybody who jumps out of airplanes all the time— on purpose—well, it takes a lot to keep a man like that amused."

Lou stared at her. "He better hope I see him before you do, huh?"

"He's got no business being so careless with that little girl's heart, Lou. She doesn't deserve it."

"I know that. And God'll get him for it. Or *I* will."

Corey stayed busy, and by the end of the week some of her annoyance had dissipated, in spite of the fact that neither she nor Lou had heard from Beltran. And there was still the nagging concern that something might have happened to him.

No, she thought. More than likely he was off doing that poker-whiskey-wild-women thing someplace and not the least bit concerned that people might be worried about him or that a little girl might be standing at the screen door watching for his hot little red car. There was only one thing Corey could do. She would take herself off that waiting list right now. She was not going to waste her great expectations on somebody like him. She and Shorty both could do without him.

She had to go to the grocery store. It seemed she *always* had to go to the grocery store for something. Shopping with a baby translated into an almost daily return trip to buy whatever she'd forgotten when she was there the first time. Shorty was reserved and watchful about most things, but she was never hesitant about whatever she could reach on a grocery store shelf, all of which she was never willing to put back again. It had become a matter of Corey's having to steer the cart mid-aisle, traveling fast, grabbing what she needed in passing, and wheeling out again—before the little fingers managed to snag fifty bags, cans or packages of something they either didn't need or couldn't afford. All in all it had become quite an adventure.

It was also the reason she didn't notice Beltran—or his...friend—until it was too late. She couldn't backtrack; she could only push on.

She nodded politely to him when he saw her, because *she* wasn't the jerk—*he* was. "Hello," she added to the young woman who was with him. She noted with some satisfaction that he had the decency to look startled at finding her and Shorty here. She tried to wheel nonchalantly past—but now Shorty had seen something in the grocery store she *really* wanted.

Him.

She held up both little arms to him, and he would have actually taken her if Corey had let him.

"Excuse us," she said. "We're in a hurry."

She tried to keep going. Shorty, in an eloquent fit of pique, snagged a bag of noodles in passing and gave it a sling. Corey made no attempt to pick it up.

"We *have* to go, baby face," she whispered. "Really, we do—this is not a good situation for you." But Shorty began to wail, bottom lip turned down and trembling.

"Matt, what—" the girlfriend said.

"I'll be right back," he said. "Mrs. Madsen, wait," he called after her. "Corey! Wait!"

"Shorty, please. Oh—I know, I know," Corey said. "It's *him*. I can see that. But you don't understand. He's—"

She glanced over her shoulder.

"Okay, okay, okay," Corey said, lifting the baby out of the cart and abandoning it in the aisle. "I get it. He's not much, but he's all you've got. Now this is how it is. I'm upset with him. And I do *not* want to talk to him until I get over it."

She looked over her shoulder again. He was right behind her.

"Wait!" he said.

"What is it, Beltran?" she said without stopping.

"I've been busy, okay?" he said before she could accuse him of anything, trying to keep up with her and not run into the oncoming carts.

"Okay," she said agreeably.

"I've been busy, damn it!"

"Yes, I can see that." She grabbed two jars of meat sticks off the shelf and kept going.

"What? You think I don't have a personal life?"

"You just don't get it, do you, Sergeant? When you take on the responsibility of a child, you no longer have the luxury of a personal life."

"You are really angry, aren't you?" he said, side-stepping two little boys carrying numerous cereal boxes. He followed her right into the express line.

She handed the checkout girl the jars of meat sticks and turned to look at him.

"No," she said. "I'm not. I'm disappointed. Most of the time I am really good at seeing through people. *Really* good. But you fooled me, Beltran. And what's worse," she said, nodding at Shorty, "you fooled *her*. What do you think all this is about? Don't you see how crazy she is about you? How glad she is to see you? Did you think you could just cut out and she wouldn't notice? Please, don't do her any more favors. Don't pretend you care about her when you don't. If you can't give her what she needs, just...stay away. Please! She's got to learn what her mother didn't. She's got to learn not to *ever* depend on men like you. Now if you'll excuse us, this baby girl and I have better things to do."

Chapter Seven

This is not working.

It was one thing when it was his idea to stay away so he could sort through this fatherhood business. It was something else entirely when his presence was no longer wanted.

Flamed in the grocery store.

Corey Madsen couldn't have put it any plainer, and he read her loud and clear. The welcome mat—as far as she was concerned—was no longer out.

He was on duty until noon, and as soon as he was relieved, he got into his car and drove to Corey's place, without ever really making the conscious decision to do so. Her station wagon wasn't in the driveway. He stopped and got out anyway. He stood in the yard, then picked up the little orange and red plastic lawn mower Shorty liked to push around and set it on the porch.

Don't do her any more favors.

"Well, well, well. Look who's here."

He looked around to find Buck standing at the edge of the yard.

"Buck," he said, acknowledging the old man's presence.

They stared at each other. Matt looked away first.

"You picked a hell of a time to get cold feet, son," Buck said.

Matt started to deny it, but that was exactly what had happened. He had gotten cold feet—and there had been nobody around to shove him out the jump door.

"You missed the party," Buck said.

"What party?"

"Shorty's belated birthday party. They finally found her birth certificate. Last Tuesday was her big fourteen months birthday—I'll wait," he added.

"For what?"

"For you to count back to see if she's yours."

Matt didn't say anything, and he didn't need to count.

"It was a great party," Buck went on. "Except for that one, very conspicuous empty chair. Everybody who is anybody was there—almost."

"Okay, I get the picture."

"No, son. I don't think you do. But I'm going to stay out of it. I *am*," he said when Matt shook his head. "Mrs. Rafferty insists. 'Don't make me hurt you, Buck.' That's how she put it when I started over here."

Matt smiled in spite of the misery he felt. "So," he said. He bent over and picked up a pinecone that was lying on the walk. "Do you...know where Corey is?"

"Yep."

"Are you going to tell me?" he asked, tossing the pinecone aside.

"I don't think so. The consensus of opinion around here is that we're better off without you— except for Shorty, of course. She's still in your corner, but then she doesn't know what it takes to make a proper father. You always park at that same place right there—and, you know, she'll climb up and try to see out the window or the door in case your car is out there. I bet she does it ten times a day. Now that's hard to watch—sweet little child like that...hoping—"

"I thought you were going to stay out of it."

"I am. If I wasn't, I'd knock you down. Right here. Right now—even if I have got forty years on you. You know what your trouble is?"

"Somehow I think you're going to tell me."

"You're not paying attention, Matt. That's what happens to most of us. We keep missing things— people—that would really enrich our lives because we just don't pay attention. And when we finally do catch on—well, then, they're gone. I've lived long enough to know that opportunity doesn't knock. The son of a bitch tries to sneak past so you can't catch him—"

"Buck," he interrupted. "Where is she? I need to talk to her."

"You going to apologize?"

"I—yeah. Okay. I'm going to apologize."

"Ain't no need to."

"What do you mean?"

"The arrangement for visitations is between you and the Department of Social Services. Corey has to honor whatever the two of you have worked out—and she doesn't have to like it. You don't have to apologize to her. Now, of course, if you wanted to say you were sorry because you know you caused *her* a certain amount of distress—well, that would be different. See, when you just quit coming, she didn't know if something happened to you or if maybe you got sent someplace where you'd be in danger again or what. When her husband, Jacob, died, it was sudden, unexpected. She never got to prepare for it, never even saw it coming. And when that happens to you once—well, you always get all worried and think the worst about things from then on, you know? And she was upset on Shorty's behalf, too. She loves that baby and she doesn't want anybody to hurt her, not even her could-be daddy." He held up his hand when Matt was about to interrupt. "I know you've got a lot to work out for yourself, and that's fine—up to a point. But you can't forget you got this little child waiting for you to get it together. Everything you do affects her. Anyway, if all *that* matters to you—well then, I guess it would be good to apologize."

Matt looked at him for a long moment. "I am *so* glad you decided to mind your own damned business," he said sarcastically, and Buck laughed.

"So...what happened to him? To Corey's husband?" Matt asked after a moment.

"Car accident. He was attending a church conference up in the mountains. When he was on his way back, a drunk driver crossed the center line and hit him. He lived for a little while afterward, but not long enough for Corey to get there.'' The old man sighed. ''That was a terrible time for our Corey—still is. Jacob was a good man.''

Unlike some others we could mention, Matt thought.

''Will Corey be back soon or not?'' he asked abruptly.

''No. She won't. She and Shorty are over at the church. Chicken pie supper. Those things last as long as the pie holds out—could be *days.* Well, there's Mrs. Rafferty,'' he said, because his wife had come out on the porch. ''Got to go before she gets a stick after me.''

''Buck,'' he called after him. ''What church is it?''

''It's not that hard to find out, son,'' Buck called back. ''If you really want to know.''

The old man disappeared inside, and Matt stood for a moment before he made up his mind. He had two choices here: start looking for chicken pie suppers, or forget it. Either one had the potential for a certain amount of misery.

He went back to the grocery store, primarily because he remembered seeing those handmade Day-Glo posters taped in the window near the entrance, the ones that advertised car washes and bazaars and things like that. He found two suppers going on today—only one selling chicken pies. He checked the windows again to make sure he hadn't missed any other posters, then went inside, circling until he found the floral department. As he walked back to the express line, he realized immediately that there was something about a paratrooper carrying a bouquet of flowers that the civilian public found intensely interesting. He tried to ignore the steady parade of grins.

"Hoo-ah!" a little old man in a running suit said to him in front of the cantaloupes.

Conspicuous now to the point of pain, Matt got in line to wait his turn, still holding his daisies and whatever the hell else they were, but he wasn't happy about it. There was just no military way to pull this off, and the entire scenario was decidedly worse than buying kitten books.

The checkout girl kept staring at him.

"What?" he said when he'd had enough.

"You were in here last night," she said.

"So?" he asked, irked now beyond human endurance.

She looked at the bouquet, then at him, and then at the bouquet again. "So you're going to need a whole lot more flowers than *that.*"

He found the church easily enough, and Corey's car. He parked close to it and got out, then toyed briefly with the idea of tossing the flowers into the nearest garbage can.

No way in hell, he decided. He'd suffered to get those things for her and he was going to give them to her—whether she wanted them or not.

All the activity seemed to center around a long brick building that was separate from the church itself. He walked in that direction, and he wasn't the only army personnel on the premises—just the only one with daisies. When he went inside, he saw Corey immediately. She was standing behind a long table cutting pieces of cake. She didn't see him, but Shorty did, and she came toddling in his direction. She was wearing some kind of little yellow bib-overall, ruffly knee pant things, and she was one good-looking baby.

"Hey, Short Stuff, how's it going?" he said, picking her up. She immediately reached out one finger to carefully touch the petals on the daisies.

"F'ower," she said, and he grinned.

"Roger that," he said. "Can't fool you, can I? Let's go see Corey, okay?" He carried her in Corey's direction, and when she looked up and saw him he thought for a moment that she was going to run. It was a very good thing he had Shorty in one arm, or she would have. She kept giving him furtive little glances as he approached, apparently trying to decide whether or not she could effectively ignore him.

He stopped at the edge of the table, standing there until she looked up again.

"I'm...sorry," he said without prelude.

She glanced at him, then immediately began cutting another piece of cake.

"I mean it," he insisted. "I'm sorry."

"Go away," she whispered. "People are staring."

"Are they?" He looked around.

Yes. They were.

She abruptly moved to the far end of the table; he followed her.

"Look," he said. "I'm trying to apologize here—"

"I'm not the one you should apologize to."

"Yeah, well, *she's* not mad at me," he said, looking at Shorty.

"People are *listening!*"

"And looking," he advised her.

"Beltran—"

"I'm trying to apologize," he said again, this time loudly enough to make her wince. "I was a jerk," he added to the nearest bunch of interested little old ladies. "I was a jerk," he said to Corey, too. "You were absolutely correct. I wasn't thinking about anybody but myself. These are for you." He held out the flowers.

She didn't take them.

"F'ower," Shorty said helpfully.

"Yes, Short Stuff, that's right," he said to her. "Flower."

"Beltran—" Corey said.

"What?"

"This is very...*not* necessary."

"It's necessary to me. I want to explain—"

"I don't want to hear it—"

"Corey?" the nearest little old lady said. "Honey?"

Corey looked in her direction.

"I think I want chocolate pound cake."

"Oh—yes. Sorry, Mrs. Bee."

"And I think you ought to let him explain," Mrs. Bee added.

"Excellent suggestion," he said to Mrs. Bee.

Corey gave him a look and cut the cake.

"Really, Corey, I do," Mrs. Bee said. "I mean, it looks like he went to a lot of trouble—didn't you?" she asked him.

"Yes, ma'am," he said. "A *lot* of trouble."

"He's brought flowers and everything. When Mr. Bee brought flowers, it—"

"Your cake, Mrs. Bee," Corey said pointedly.

"Oh…well…thank you, honey."

"Yesterday at the grocery store—it wasn't what it looked like," Matt said when Mrs. Bee had at least pretended to move on. "Well, actually, it *was* what it looked like but, see, you've got to understand how the army works. When you're outranked and you're told you have to be rewarded for your outstanding performance—particularly when it makes somebody higher up look good—well, then, you have to do it. There was this damn cookout thing at the captain's house. I didn't want to go, but I did. Then they ran out of some things, so I went to get them. And I took Lucy—you saw Lucy."

"Yes," Corey said. "I saw Lucy."

"See, we had just finished this big project. It was a *lot* of work, and it—"

"Took the *whole* two weeks," Corey supplied helpfully.

"Yes, damn it, it did! I admit I could have called you or Lou or somebody and said I would be tied up until further notice, and maybe I could have come by for a little while, but I—"

"Didn't want to," Corey said, being helpful again.

"Who's telling this?"

"You are."

"Well, then, butt out."

"As I recall, *I* never wanted *in*."

He looked at her, trying not to be distracted by her

pink dress. Soft…mouth. Beautiful…sad…*disappointed* eyes.

"Okay," he said abruptly. "Here it is. Like I said before, you were absolutely correct. I didn't call because I didn't want to. I didn't come by because I didn't want to. This thing was moving way too fast for me, and I decided to bail out while I still could. But I was wrong. I seriously lost sight of the main objective here." He held Shorty up a little higher for emphasis. "And I underestimated the consequences—for her and for me. But I'm not as stupid as I look and act, and I don't think it's too late for damage control and a new plan. There is no reason why we can't regroup here. And that's all I have to say."

He waited.

And waited.

"Well, say something!"

"Thank you for the flowers," Corey said dutifully.

"Besides that."

"I think you'd better quit while you're ahead, Sergeant."

He ate chicken pie. A lot more than he wanted. And he fed Shorty. Then the two of them tried to find a way to hide the green beans that came with it, even though Mrs. Bee was the one who had donated them. He realized he was indebted to the woman for the good word she had put in for him, but these were, after all, *green beans*.

"What are you two up to?" Corey said at one point.

"Nothing," he assured her.

"Give me those things before you cause me any more trouble than you already have."

He was only too happy to let her make the beans disappear, in spite of the fact that he didn't quite follow what she meant by the remark. What kind of trouble had he caused? The church was making money off him. He had *paid* for the chicken pie, *and* the damn green beans, for that matter. He and Shorty were both behaving satisfactorily, by almost anyone's standards, and they really were trying to be discreet about their mutual aversion to beans.

But Corey didn't give him time to ask for clarification. She whisked the beans away and went back to cutting cake. He continued to hang out with Shorty and chatted with the customers and the volunteers, several privates, a corporal or two, and a choir director. And he watched Corey. He would say one thing for her. Given the half-drowned way she looked the first time he'd seen her, she certainly cleaned up good. He did like that pink dress. And the way he could *almost* see the tops of her breasts at the neckline. And the way her hair was kind of mussed and just-out-of-bed looking. And the *legs*.

What he didn't like was the man who kept coming over to talk to her. Thirty-, maybe forty-something, slightly balding, grinning. He was a Yuppie, an expensive-college alumni-type, the kind who said, "Super!" all the time. And clearly, he was exceptionally witty, given the number of times he made her smile.

Smile, Matt suddenly thought. Not laugh. If anything, the smile looked a little strained.

And he understood, from the reciprocal look the Yuppie gave him, that he was pretty much wondering the same thing about the sergeant. No, indeed. The Yuppie wasn't exactly thrilled that Matt had crashed the chicken pie supper, flowers in hand, and was now carrying around one of Corey Madsen's favorite people.

"Who is that guy?" he said to Shorty.

"F'ower," the favorite person answered.

"He's going to get 'f'owered' if he's not careful."

It was only as he said it that he realized he was actually suffering from an extreme attack of jealousy. He didn't want the man talking to Corey Madsen. He didn't want the man even looking at her. And where did *that* come from? He wasn't the jealous type. He'd never been jealous over a woman in his life.

Never.

He volunteered to police the area with a trash bag so he could get closer to their conversation. He and Shorty picked up discarded paper plates and napkins all around, but he was never able to hear what the man said to Corey. He had to content himself with trying to look as if he didn't notice and therefore couldn't possibly mind. Which he didn't—or, more accurately, shouldn't.

Oh, yeah. Everything is just super.

Unfortunately, the trip around the room with the trash bag opened the door for Mrs. Bee to volunteer him for other details—pot washing, can opening, cake carrying. The cake carrying he didn't mind, because of the ultimate destination.

"You want me to take Shorty?" Corey asked when he presented her with another pound cake, because he'd been more or less wearing the kid ever since he arrived.

"No, she's fine," he said. He tried not to stare at her, but he couldn't help it. "What's wrong?" he finally asked, because he saw no point in avoiding the bottom line. She looked tired, maybe upset—but not upset the way she had been with him earlier. This was different, and it was all too familiar. A soldier-running-on-empty look.

"I was about to ask you the same thing," she said.

"No, I mean it. What's wrong?"

"Nothing," she said. She gave him a small smile that was even worse than the ones she'd been handing out to the Yuppie. And she took Shorty anyway.

Mrs. Bee was calling him—again. He went to see what she wanted, but he kept looking at Corey and the baby instead of listening.

"This is the first time," Mrs. Bee said.

"What?" he asked, because he had no idea what she was talking about and couldn't pretend that he did.

"Since Jacob died," Mrs. Bee said. "This is the first time Corey's come to one of these suppers. I think it's really hard for her. I mean, it's like he's just going to walk in that door any minute. Did you know Jacob?"

"Ah, no, ma'am. I didn't."

"He was a fine man," she said.

"So I've heard."

"That's his picture over there on that wall. Have you seen it?"

"No," he said. He took a quiet breath and willed Shorty to fret or something so he could make an excuse to go over there and get her.

"I was thinking, Sergeant..." She squinted in an attempt to read his name tag.

"Beltran," he reminded her.

"I was thinking, Sergeant Beltran..." She looked up at him.

Here it comes, he thought. *The let-the-widow-grieve-in-peace speech.*

"Maybe you might see if you could get Corey to go on home."

"You think that's a good idea?" he asked, completely surprised by the suggestion.

"Yes," she said. "I do. This place is too full of memories for her, and Ted keeps bothering her."

"Ted?"

"The politician. He's a nice enough man, I guess—for somebody in his line of work. And he's got a lot of money from his mama's side of the family, but—" She lowered her voice. "He's not very subtle. I don't think Corey likes him."

"You don't?"

"No. I think all the memories *and* Ted are just about too much for her. I think she should leave now." She smiled. "And I think *you* can get her to do it."

Mrs. Bee walked away without waiting for him to comment. He looked across the room at Corey. He wasn't exactly known for subtlety himself, but he was certainly willing to give this thing a whirl.

Okay, Mrs. Bee, he thought as he walked in Corey's direction. *Can do.*

But Shorty had fallen asleep on Corey's shoulder, and she had already decided to leave without any coaxing from him.

"I'm going to take Shorty home," she said. "She's had about all the chicken pie doings she can handle."

He reached out and stroked the baby's soft head, thinking, as he always did, what a beautiful little girl she was.

"Is it okay if I stop by the house for a minute?" he asked, surprising them both. He doubted if Mrs. Bee had had this in mind, but what the hell.

Corey's eyes briefly met his, but she didn't say anything.

"There are a couple of things I want to run by you," he said. "If it's not too late or anything."

He could see the struggle she was having trying to decide if she could deal with any more of his intrusion, and he willed himself not to push it.

"Okay," she said finally.

"Where's your gear?"

"My gear?"

"The diaper...bag thing." But Mrs. Bee, whose confidence in his powers of persuasion apparently knew no bounds, was already bringing it.

"Would you get my flowers?" Corey asked him.

He picked them up off the cake table, more pleased that she actually wanted his grocery store flowers than he would have ever admitted. And as he was walking out, it occurred to him, that carrying flowers still didn't do much to enhance the warrior image. Carrying flowers *and* a diaper bag pretty much killed it altogether.

He helped put Shorty into the car seat, and he followed Corey home. He carried the baby inside the house and, with Corey's permission, he put her to bed.

He was surprised that she didn't stay to supervise, and he didn't see her when he came out of the baby's room. The house was still dark except for a small lamp in the hall and a fluorescent light in the kitchen.

He went looking for her in there. She had put the flowers into a blue vase and left them sitting on the kitchen counter. He walked carefully around the table and the high chair and went into the large den. She was standing on the far side near the French doors that led out onto a side porch.

He realized after a moment that there was music playing softly, classical music—Mozart or somebody like that. He stood still, not knowing quite what to do. He was in alien territory here. Holy Angels had taught him all about church suppers, but he'd had no experience with highbrow music in the dark.

He did know about grief, however, and he supposed he would have to use that as a frame of reference.

"It's going to rain," she said.

He walked closer. "Is it?"

A faint rumble of thunder answered his question.

"Everything's squared away with Shorty. I think she had a good time tonight," he said.

"*You* were there," she said simply.

"Buck said they found her birth certificate." He blundered on, because he still was on unfamiliar ground here. "I guess you know her name now."

She turned to him. She was hardly a step away, but he couldn't see her face. He could smell the soft scent that was her. It was like…fresh air and sunshine and citrus and evergreen all at the same time.

"Olivia," she said. "Her name is Olivia Warren. It fits her, doesn't it? Intelligent and assertive—but feminine. Nobody pushes an 'Olivia' around."

He didn't say anything. The name didn't surprise him. Rita lived in a fantasy world and collected fine porcelain teacups. Teacups and "Olivia" went together, to his way of thinking.

The conversation lagged. She stood there, her arms crossed over her breasts as if she were cold. He could feel her looking at him in the dark. He systematically abandoned any of a number of the bogus reasons he might have given for wanting to come by here. There was nothing he really needed to talk to her about. He had only wanted to stay with her as long as he could.

"Well, I guess I'd better go," he said, and he would have, but she reached out to stop him. He stood there, with her hand on his arm, waiting.

"Are you sure you're all right?" he asked.

"Yes," she said. "I…" She bowed her head. Her hand remained on his arm, warm, soft. He had *no* idea where this had come from—or where it was going.

He heard her give a wavering sigh, and she was leaning into him suddenly. He could feel her breasts against his chest. Incredibly, her arms slid upward around his neck and she lifted her face to his.

What is this?

He didn't care what it was. The awkwardness he had been feeling suddenly translated into fierce desire. His mouth brushed against hers. His hand found her breast. She gave a soft moan, her breath warm and sweet against his cheek.

Trembling. He was trembling. He hadn't even kissed her yet. His arms tightened around her.

Oh, God.

He could feel how much she wanted—needed.

Jacob.

Maybe she hadn't actually said his name. It didn't matter. Matt felt him, too—with everything that was in him—and there was no mistaking it.

Jacob.

She was clinging to him, but he took her by her shoulders and held her away from him.

"No," he said. "No. There are a lot of things I would do for you, but letting you pretend I'm your dead husband isn't one of them."

Chapter Eight

She didn't expect to see Beltran again. Ever. Whether she was looking after his child or not. He had failed to appear before—and with much less provocation than she had given him.

She could hardly bear to think about it. She had actually...would have actually—

No matter how hard she tried not to, she remembered everything.

Everything.

The way he smelled. The way his strong body felt against hers. Before, she had always thought of herself as shy when it came to that kind of thing. She never *initiated.* Even with Jacob she hadn't. She had no excuse whatsoever for her behavior with Beltran.

None.

How could I have done that?

It was a question she asked herself over and over, and she was very much afraid she knew the answer. As much as she had loved Jacob, as deep in mourning as she had been, she wanted Mateo Beltran.

And she hadn't seen him as some kind of stand-in. He had been mistaken about that. It wasn't just that she was missing Jacob and Beltran was a warm body that happened to be there. If that was all she required, there was the incredibly persistent Ted, who cornered her at every opportunity with his pseudo-empathy for her widowhood and his innuendos as to his availability. *He* would have been only too happy to accommodate her sexual needs. No, it was Beltran himself who intrigued her. She thought about him all the time, about his life in the military and about when he was a boy growing up in an orphanage. Who had comforted him when he was sick or afraid? Who had looked out for him? Someone must have, because he was a good man. He was a little rough around the edges, but he was still a kind person. She hadn't been brought up to expect that of a man who went to topless bars and got drunk and fathered illegitimate children. But she had recognized it in him from the beginning. When he had all but thrown the money at her to buy the baby some shoes. When he refused to let that young soldier—Santos— be harassed because she cried when she had to make a jump.

And when he refused to let me make a fool of myself, she thought.

Oh, yes, she had wanted him, and she would have given in to that misguided desire, if *he* hadn't put a stop to it. There was no use trying to convince herself otherwise.

On the day of his next scheduled visit, she woke up tense and nervous and she stayed that way. But, incredibly, he arrived exactly when he was supposed to, cheerful and laughing. He talked to Shorty and showed no fear whatsoever that the pitiful and sexually deprived Widow Madsen would once again try to crawl all over him. He might not be willing to let her pretend that he was Jacob, but he was clearly determined to let her pretend that her little moment of weakness had never happened. She appreciated it, but it was all she could do to look him in the face.

The day was warm, and he took Shorty outside. Corey had the windows open, and she could hear them "talking"—his deep voice and Shorty's mostly unintelligible gibberish. She couldn't help it. She moved to where she could see them from time to time. He was so good with her. He had been telling the truth when he said that he knew about children. She supposed that he'd been surrounded by motherless, abandoned children his whole life, and, for all intents and purposes, he still was.

Shorty was engaged now in her favorite outside activity—noisily "mowing" the carpet of pine needles in the front yard with her toy mower. And though she constantly got herself and the mower hung up on the uneven terrain, Beltran didn't physically help her out of the predicament but encouraged her out of it.

"Outstanding!" he'd tell her when she was on the move again. "Now you say, 'Too easy, Sergeant!'"

Corey smiled. One of these days Shorty *would* say

it, and Corey fervently hoped she was on hand to see his face when it happened.

"What? We're going to drag it up the steps now? Okay. What's a couple hundred steps, right? Go! Go! What?" he said again when Shorty let out a squeal of frustration when she discovered that the idea was much easier than the execution.

"No, you do it," he said. "You do it—what?"

Corey looked outside again, because he was laughing. Shorty had him by the shirtsleeve and was pulling for dear life, trying to get him around to where she could hold on to him while she dragged the lawn mower up the steps.

"Too easy! You are one smart cookie, baby girl."

Corey moved to the French doors and stepped outside. There was no use putting this off any longer. He was sitting on the top step now, with Shorty trying to get herself and the lawn mower onto his lap. He looked around when she let the door swing closed.

"Sergeant Beltran, I..." she began.

"We're not going to go there," he said.

She frowned. "What?"

"I said we're not going to go there."

"You don't understand—"

"I don't? Look at me, Mrs. Madsen. I'm sitting here with this baby on my knee—a baby I'm nine-tenths sure is mine. If she is, then you know how I got her. You think I don't understand that sometimes you feel so bad, you do things you wouldn't normally do? If *anybody* knows that, it's me."

"Feeling bad is no excuse."

"We're not talking about excuses. We're talking about understanding."

"I'm very...ashamed."

"Yeah, well, that kind of goes with the territory."

"It was wrong of me to put you in that situation and I'm sorry. I don't want to do anything to jeopardize your relationship with Shorty or make you feel that you can't come here without—"

"Leave it *alone*, Mrs. Madsen," he said pointedly. "I mean it."

She nodded, embarrassed and relieved all at the same time. She took a quiet breath, then turned to go back inside the house.

"There's just one thing," he said, and she looked at him.

"What?"

"Don't do it again. You're an attractive woman, and I can't promise that I'll behave as honorably as I did the other night. I'm nothing like your late husband. I think you'd better remember that."

For once, she met his eyes and held his gaze for a long moment.

Actually, she thought. *You are.*

"I have to go," he said abruptly. "If you'd take the Merry Mower here..." He handed the baby over. "See you, Short Stuff," he said. "Be a good girl. Let's see you do the 'bye-bye' thing." He waved, and Shorty promptly waved back. "Outstanding."

He looked at Corey. She thought he was about to say something, but he didn't. He gave her one of his almost smiles instead. She stood with the baby and watched him drive away.

When she was about to go inside, Lou Kurian pulled into the driveway.

"Guess what, boys and girls?" she said as she got out of the car.

Corey only shook her head. She was *not* up to guessing.

"Okay," Lou said. "If it's that kind of day, let me just cut to the chase, because I'm **not** going to make it any better. I came by to tell you there have been developments. Rita Warren is back."

Corey felt the wind go out of her. "*How* back?" she asked.

"She says permanently."

"Do we believe that?"

"Well, she's established residence and she's looking for a job. She's also looking for a lawyer. She says she wants Shorty."

"Can she have her?"

"Probably—"

"Probably? What do you mean 'probably'?"

"If she gets her act together—I mean *probably*. You know how it works in this state. If at all possible, we keep the family together. If she's not a drug addict and if she's employed—well, the courts look kindly upon that. The bottom line is that, legally, she *is* the mother."

"She abandoned her baby on a military base, for God's sake."

"Yes. She did."

"Excuse me," Corey said. She turned abruptly and carried Shorty inside. She didn't realize until she reached the kitchen that Lou had come with her.

"I shouldn't have taken her," Corey said, feeling

her mouth tremble. She bit down on her lower lip. "I shouldn't have taken her, and I shouldn't have kept her."

"Corey, what's the matter with you? You've been through this before."

Not alone, Corey thought.

"It's not like you didn't know she'd have to leave sometime—"

"It's not the same," Corey said.

"Honey, it *is* the same. And it's part of the job—"

"It's not the same, Lou! I…don't think I can stand it."

"You have to think of the child, not yourself. You know that. You *said* that."

"I *am* thinking of the child! Can't you see how much she's changed? She laughs now—she's happy. She's like a beautiful flower somebody forgot to water, and she's finally blooming. I don't want her to go back to being the dirty, sad little child she was when she came here. Rita Warren is—"

"Rita Warren is her mother," Lou interrupted quietly.

And Beltran is her father, Corey suddenly thought.

"We're going to have to set up supervised visits for her," Lou said.

Corey didn't say anything.

"Did you hear me?"

"I heard you."

"Corey, you're going to have to get yourself together here. I know it's sudden. It's *always* sudden. Are you going to be okay with this?"

She didn't answer. Her throat ached. She could feel tears welling in her eyes.

"Well, you're going to have to get okay—and right quick. I don't want to have to move Shorty to another foster home because you can't handle this. How hard do you think it's going to be on *her* if you forget what the priorities are here?" Lou stopped and gave a sharp sigh. She rubbed a spot between her eyes. "Damn it. This is all *my* fault. You said you weren't ready to take a child. I didn't do you any favors by forcing you into this situation, did I?"

Corey didn't say anything. She glanced at Shorty, who was on the verge of crying with her, and she abruptly smiled.

"It's okay," she whispered, giving the baby a kiss and a hug. "You don't have to worry. I just forgot something, that's all. I forgot your mommy loves you, too."

She could feel Lou looking at her, and she finally glanced in her direction.

"Okay," she said. "I'm okay."

"You sure?"

"I'm sure. I just—I'm really crazy about this baby, you know?"

"You always have gotten attached to the children who stayed here," Lou said. "You can't do it any other way."

"And I always had Jacob to lean on after they were gone."

"Like I said, I didn't do you any favors. I did *her* one."

Corey forced a smile. "I hope so. Well—that's that. You let me know when the visit is." Shorty abruptly laid her head on Corey's shoulder, and she gently rubbed the baby's back.

"I admire you," Lou said. "I admire you and I appreciate you."

"And you're on the verge of sounding like a beer commercial."

Lou laughed. "I've got to go."

"Lou, one more thing."

"What?"

"Beltran. Is he really Shorty's father or not?"

"Now, Corey, you know I can't discuss that. And even if he is, he's not an acceptable alternative. You can't give custody to somebody who's liable to be off to war any second. I'll call you when the visit with Rita is all set."

Corey was too restless to stay in the house. She was on a countdown now, and she and Shorty had to enjoy themselves as much as possible in whatever time they had left. She took the baby to the mall to do some of the things she could afford—wheeling the stroller past dozens of other women with babies in strollers, talking to the puppies and kittens at the pet store, and actually buying some chocolate chip cookies. When there was nothing else left to do but sit on one of the benches, she and the baby went home. They had a quiet supper, and after the mall and the mowing, Shorty was only too happy to have a bath and be put to bed.

Corey lay down on the sofa, alone in the dark, listening to the adagio from Rodrigo's *Concierto de Aranjuez*. She didn't really feel tired. She didn't feel anything, and she recognized that particular survival skill immediately. She had become an expert at *not* feeling since Jacob died.

Just don't think about it. Don't.

But she did think about it. About frightened little Shorty in her too small shoes and her dirty clothes.

No, not Shorty. Beltran's little girl.

Olivia.

I'm not her mother, she thought, and wishing wouldn't make it so. She wasn't anything—just the temporary caregiver. At least, that was all she had intended to be.

But a child's trust was an awesome thing, and this baby had come to trust her without reservation. Corey knew exactly what would happen on the morning Lou came to take her away. Unsuspecting little Shorty would eagerly go to her, smiling and happy, and she wouldn't realize until the last moment, perhaps when Lou had already put her into the car, that Corey wasn't coming, too. She wouldn't understand what was happening, and suddenly she'd be afraid. She'd hold out her hands to be taken, but Corey would have to just stand there as the car backed out of the drive. And the last thing she would see was the look on Shorty's face—all that trust dying away.

I have to let her go. I have to.

Oh, God, how am I going to stand it?

The self-imposed apathy she had felt earlier suddenly gave way, and she closed her eyes and began to cry.

She hadn't intended to fall asleep, but she awoke suddenly to the ringing of the telephone. Her head ached from crying, and she had no idea what time it was. She fumbled for the receiver without turning the light on.

"Hello?" she said, her voice husky and strange-sounding.

"Corey? It's me."

She raised up on one elbow. "Beltran? What—"

"I'm going," he said.

"Going? Going where?"

"I don't know."

"Well...when will you be back?"

"I don't know."

She didn't say anything.

"Do you understand?" he asked after a moment.

"No," she said truthfully, still trying to wake up and wondering why he would call her in the middle of the night to *not* tell her something.

"Shorty's okay?" he asked.

"Yes, she's fine. Beltran—"

"I'll see you when I get back."

"Wait...wait, I want to ask you something."

"What?"

"Rita Warren—what is she like?"

"What?" he said again.

"I want to know what she's like. Tell me. Please..."

"Are you sure you're awake?"

"I'm awake. Tell me."

"She's—hell, I don't know. Why are you asking me this? I've told you about her."

"Is she a bad person?"

"Bad? No, she's not *bad,* I guess. She just doesn't know any better. She's got family, but she pretty much raised herself. She doesn't visit them much because she said they'd steal everything she's got. She lives in this big fantasy world. She dreams about being a showgirl in one of the big-name casinos in Las Vegas or a movie star or something like that.''

"Beltran, what kind of mother is she? Was she good to—''

"Corey, I've got to go," he interrupted.

She could hear a lot of commotion in the background—metal things clanging and men's voices.

"You and Shorty take care of yourselves," he said.

"Beltran—''

She intended to tell him to be careful, but he hung up before she got the chance. She lay there in the dark, still clutching the receiver, fully aware of the feelings she *hadn't* intended to share with him.

Chapter Nine

It was taking her a long time to come to the door. He considered that she might not be able to hear him over the rain, or that she might be busy with the baby, or that she might not be home, even if her car was in the driveway.

He was just about to give up when the door abruptly opened. She was surprised to see him, he could tell that much. And if he read her right, she was at least a little bit glad.

"You're back," she said, opening the screen door.

"Not much to it," he said, stepping out of the rain and into the warmth of her smile. "Never got beyond the saber rattling."

There was no doubt that *he* was glad to see her. He tried not to stare at her, though staring was safer, he supposed, than doing what he actually wanted to do.

I am in deep trouble here, he thought. He had suspected as much the whole time he was gone. Now he was absolutely certain, and he had no idea what to do about it.

"How's Shorty?" he asked, trying to keep his eyes on her face and not on her breasts. She was wearing jeans and a little V-neck T-shirt. Some kind of soft...baby blue thing with a ribbon bow pretty much where he—

Don't look, damn it!

"She's had a virus—some fever and an upset stomach. She's better, though. She's napping. When did you get back?" She led the way into the kitchen, and he was only too happy to follow. Something smelled great. Baking bread, he guessed.

And something looked great—her.

Oh, man, I missed this.

"I've been back awhile," he said.

Like, oh, forty-five minutes.

"Where were you?"

"First one place and then another," he said, still trying to sneak a look at whatever he could and not drool. He wanted to make love with her so *bad.* He wanted to be as close to her as he could get. He wanted feel her body against his, around his. He wanted to watch her eyes while he took her. He wanted her to say his name.

His name.

And then he wanted to let her rest for a minute and do it all over again. He nearly smiled. The fantasy had gotten pretty exaggerated in the past few weeks.

"Have you ever thought of transferring to the

CIA?'' she asked, looking over her shoulder. "I can never get a straight answer out of you.''

"Can't you?'' he asked, smiling broadly now.

"You know I can't.''

"Well, if you can't, nobody can,'' he said.

"Exactly.'' She laughed.

"So what's new?''

The minute he asked the question, her smile faded. He thought for a minute she was going to cry.

"You...haven't talked to Lou, I guess,'' she said.

"No. Why? Is something wrong?''

"It all depends.''

"On what?''

"On whether you're Rita Warren or...me. Are you hungry?'' she asked abruptly.

"No—yes. What are you talking about? What about Rita?''

"I've got the perennial rainy-day favorite—potato soup.''

"Corey, what's going on?'' he said, catching her by the arm to keep her from running off and stirring a pot.

"Let's eat, okay?'' she said, stepping out of his grasp. "I haven't had anything all day. We'll eat and then we'll talk.''

He stood there, wondering if this was some ritual she had established with Jacob, one where she tried to postpone dealing with a major problem by hauling out the comfort food. And this problem was major. He could look at her and tell that.

But he was hungry—and in no particular hurry to hear any kind of bad news. He certainly could live with the prospect of having a home-cooked meal, especially with her. "Okay," he said.

She immediately turned away to get the bowls.

He made himself at home. He went to wash his hands, and it occurred to him when he glanced at his bleary-eyed and unshaven image in the bathroom mirror that no one could accuse him of getting his beauty sleep. It was a wonder Corey had even opened the door.

He went in to see Shorty and stood watching her quiet breathing for a time. She had grown. He'd been gone three weeks, and he could literally see how much she'd grown.

Sweet little Olivia.

Your old man's home, Short Stuff.

He smiled abruptly. When she woke up, maybe they could crack open a jar of meat sticks to celebrate.

He returned to the kitchen, and Corey had the table set. He helped with the bread and the cheese, so he could get closer to her, so he could reach across her, touch her skin, smell her hair.

She was good at keeping whatever was bothering her under wraps until she was ready to talk about it. They ate in silence, the only sounds the rain beating against the windowpane, and the radio playing softly—the FM "oldies" station. He didn't try to initiate any small talk. He just...waited.

"Rita Warren is back," she said finally.

He looked up at her. She wasn't kidding.

"And?"

"And she's got a job and a lawyer, and more than likely, she's going to get Shorty, too."

"Yeah? For how long? Until she decides to dump her in somebody's car again? What does Lou say?"

"Lou says the court will probably let her have her child back."

"Shorty isn't just *her* child. She's mine, too."

She looked at him a moment. He supposed it was because he'd never been so definite about it before.

"You don't count," she said finally.

"I don't *count?* She left the kid with me and totally disappeared. I counted then, didn't I? It's not my fault I didn't even know Shorty existed. I took the paternity test and I passed it with flying colors. I've been doing everything Lou and the department says I need to do. Yeah, yeah, I know. The going was a little bumpy at first, but I'm getting there." He abruptly got up from the table and stood looking out the window at the rain. "This is not good. I don't want Shorty to go back with her, damn it!"

"I checked with a lawyer...on your behalf," she said quietly.

He looked at her. "What lawyer?"

"Ted Bingham—"

"Ted? The politician-at-the-chicken-pie-supper Ted?"

"Yes."

"I didn't think you liked him."

"I don't—how did you know that?"

"Never mind. What did you tell him—on my behalf?"

"Everything."

"Well, great, Corey. Maybe I didn't want you to tell the son of a bitch *everything*. Did you think of that?"

"No, I didn't," she said. "I was desperate to find an alternative."

"Well, I hope you found one."

She took a quiet breath. "Ted says there's really only one thing you can do."

"And what is that?"

"Get married."

He laughed. "Now *there's* a solution. I don't suppose he said who I could get married *to?*"

"He said it would have to be somebody with a good reputation—"

"Nobody from the topless bars, then."

"I'm serious, Beltran."

"So am I."

"And she'd have to be someone willing to raise a child you had with another woman."

"I hope he didn't charge you for this excellent advice—"

"Beltran, do you want to hear this or not?"

"I want to hear something that at least makes some sense, Mrs. Madsen. And so far old Ted's batting zero."

"No, he isn't."

"Yes, he is."

"Matt, would you consider..."

He looked at her. She wouldn't quite meet his eyes.

"Don't tell me you've gone out and found a respectable, marriage-minded woman for me," he said.

"Yes. I have."

"Who?"

"Me," she said.

He laughed. "What did you say?"

"You heard me."

"No, I don't think I did. I think I've got a bad case of jet lag, and you—I don't know what the hell is wrong with *you.*"

"Nothing is wrong with me. I've told you the problem and I've told you the only solution I could find. And now I'm asking you to marry me. For Shorty's sake. It's as simple as that. We can get married, and then you can petition the court—"

"Hold it! I have one small question here."

"What is it?"

"Are you out of your mind?"

"No, I don't think so. I just…love your daughter. I didn't intend to get so emotionally involved in her—your—situation, but I—" She broke off and gave a quiet sigh. "The truth is, it would break my heart if she had to go back to the way she was before she came here."

"So you would actually do it? *You* would marry *me?*"

"To keep Shorty, yes."

"Do you have any idea what people would say?"

"What people?"

"Your people—the church people, your family, the people at Social Services, your friends, Jacob's family, *Ted*—" He considered the list impressive already, and he had left out the express-lane checkout girl at the supermarket.

"It's none of their business."

He sat down at the table again. She must have given this a lot of thought, because she was so damned…*serene* about the whole thing. He could not *believe* they were having this conversation.

"I think we'd get along fine," she said.

"You do."

"Yes, I do."

"Why?"

"Because I would make that a priority."

"Meaning what? You'd be really careful not to tell me to go to hell when I needed it?"

"No," she said pointedly. "You'd have to...behave."

He smiled. "Behave? No whiskey or cards or wild women, I guess?"

"For starters," she said. "And any complaints I had, you'd know about. And I'd expect the same from you. I know it may be difficult for you to imagine what it's like if you've never been married—or have you?"

"No. I haven't. You see how crazy this is? You don't know anything about me."

"Well, it's not for lack of trying," she said. "Anyway, I know what I need to know."

"Which is?"

"Well, it's kind of hard to put into words."

"Yeah, I'll just bet."

"I think—" She looked into his eyes. "No, I *know* you would never deliberately hurt me or Shorty. Ever."

Her remark caught him completely off guard. He didn't know what to say or how she could possibly voice something that he himself had only just realized.

"Do you have any idea how hard it is to be a military wife?" he asked.

"I know how hard it is to be a pastor's wife," she said. "It can't be much more difficult."

He frowned. Somehow he hadn't expected that particular comparison.

"So what kind of arrangement are you offering?" he asked.

She gave a slight shrug. "A good home—for the three of us."

"Here," he said.

"Yes, here."

"In Jacob's house."

"It's not Jacob's house. It's my house. It belonged to my grandmother. When she died, she left it to me. It was always a happy place for me, and I wanted to live in it instead of a church parsonage. Actually, Jacob didn't like it all that much."

"Why not?"

"The house needed a lot of work. It still does. And the neighborhood isn't very good."

"Looks fine to me."

"Then you'd be willing to live here?"

"Let's not get ahead of ourselves, Mrs. Madsen. So tell me, exactly what are we talking about here? For better or worse and all that?"

"Yes."

"For keeps, too."

"Yes."

"Would this be a marriage of…convenience, or what? Something legal, but in name only?"

"No," she said, and he laughed again.

"I don't think that's funny," she said, blushing.

"You can't see your face."

"I don't know what you mean."

"I mean, I might believe you if you didn't look like a jump school trainee two seconds from getting shoved out the door."

"I think you've forgotten the other night," she said quietly.

"That didn't have a damn thing to do with me, and we both know it. That was you missing your husband."

She didn't say anything.

"What if I wanted more children?" he asked bluntly.

She looked at him steadily. "Then I guess you have to...marry someone else."

"I see. You want to raise my kid, but you wouldn't want to *have* my kid. Right?"

She started to get up from the table, then didn't. "It's not that I wouldn't be...willing to do it," she said in that earnest and altogether believable way she had. "It's that I don't think I could. I had three miscarriages, and the doctors never could give me a real reason why. Unless you count 'sometimes it's just for the best' as a diagnosis. Jacob came from a big family. He wanted children very much. A lot of children. But I just couldn't...try anymore. It hurt too much to keep losing babies and know it's your fault. It was...difficult for him."

"Not as difficult as it was for you," he said, and he would have been hard-pressed to identify the look she gave him.

"I haven't put this very well," she said.

"I understand what's going on."

"What's...going on?"

"Yeah. You said you love Shorty, right? You love

her enough to do whatever it takes to keep her safe and to give her a chance for a good life—even marry me. Yes or no?''

"Yes," she said, looking into his eyes again.

"Yes," he repeated.

"I know you need some time to think about this—"

"No, actually, I don't," he said.

"You don't?"

"No."

"Oh," she said, her disappointment obvious.

"Based on what I've seen, 'love' isn't much of a reason to get married these days—at least, it's not a long-term one. But who knows? Maybe giving a kid a home is. I guess it…deserves some consideration. I'll think about it."

His answer was evasive at best, but she still looked at him as if it was much more than she had expected.

"What?" he asked. "Changed your mind already?"

She took a deep breath and gave him an embarrassed smile. "No, I…guess I'm just not used to having my marriage proposals…considered."

"Are you *sure* you want to do this?"

"I'm sure," she said. "There's no other way."

"When you asked me if Rita was a bad person, you knew what she was up to then, didn't you?"

"Yes."

"And you weren't going to tell me?"

"You didn't give me a chance."

"No, I guess I didn't." He leaned back in the chair. He was so tired suddenly. This had been one hell of a day.

But he had things to do, people to see. He got up from the table.

"Thanks for the home-cooked meal," he said. "It was great." He smiled slightly. "And the proposal. It wasn't half-bad, either."

"You're leaving?"

"Yeah. I want to check on Shorty first, and then I'm gone. I need to find out a few things before I—" He stopped because of the way she was looking at him. She was still worried and scared, he could see that, and he didn't know what to do about it. She had been absolutely correct. He would never deliberately hurt her, and he marveled that she could know that and yet not seem to know how much he wanted her. Hell, yes, he'd marry her. In a heartbeat. He wanted her more than he'd ever wanted any woman in his whole life. And he wanted everything that came with her—a home, a family. And she didn't have a clue.

But the key word here was "deliberately." He had no idea which would hurt her the most—marrying her or not marrying her. He had to see Miss Lou. He wanted to know how exact the paternity testing was. It was good enough for him as is, and it was good enough for the state of North Carolina, but it might not be good enough for a get-down-and-dirty custody fight. And he wanted to talk to a lawyer on his own. He needed to verify that Ted knew what he was talking about and that he wasn't just trying to keep him from crashing any more chicken pie suppers. If truth be told, he was kind of hoping that was the case. He hoped good old Ted was trying to get him out of the picture by marrying him off. In which case, good old Ted just might be in for the surprise of his life.

The baby was still sleeping. He briefly touched her cheek with his fingertips. "Short Stuff, you are *not* going to believe this," he whispered.

But she slept blissfully on, completely unaware of the abrupt one hundred and eighty degree turn her life—and his—had taken.

Corey was still sitting at the kitchen table when he returned.

"So if somebody asks me what's new, do I say I'm thinking about getting married or not?" he asked from the doorway.

"Your call," she said.

"Have you talked to your family about this?"

"Yes."

"You told them everything?"

"Not…exactly. They all know Shorty, and I just said I was planning on proposing to her father."

"Well, that must have made a few eyeballs click."

"They were…interested."

"I'm sure."

"Especially my brothers," she said, with just the slightest hint of mischievousness.

"Brothers. Like, how many brothers?"

"Oh…three," she said, trying not to smile.

"*Three?* Well, if it's only *three*…"

"One is a navy SEAL."

"And you are full of it, Madsen," he said, laughing. "So what did they say?"

"Well, two of them did question the rationality of such a venture."

"Said you were totally nuts, did they?"

"More or less. I've never been known to make marriage proposals before."

"Yeah, especially to fly-by-night military types with unclaimed children. It's a wonder they didn't try to have you committed."

"There's still time," she said.

He couldn't keep from smiling. He liked this woman. Aside from the rampant lust he was feeling—and had been for some time—he honest-to-God *liked* her.

But he had never been known to let well enough alone.

"What about Jacob's family?"

"What?" she asked, startled.

"Jacob's family. Have you told them, too?"

"I—yes."

"Wasn't that a little…premature?"

"Jacob's mother's sister asked," she said. She gave a small shrug.

"Jacob's mother's sister? Is that some kind of Madsen chain of command?"

"More or less. You came to the church supper with flowers. She heard about it, and she had…questions."

"Big ones, I guess."

"Just one big one."

"Which was?"

"I'd rather not say."

"Well, I'd rather you did."

She sighed. "She wanted to know if you and I were…carrying on."

He smiled again. "Carrying on? You and me?"

"Yes."

"And you said?"

"I said…"

"What?" he prompted when she faded under the pressure of telling him.

"I said…not yet."

He laughed out loud. "Madsen—"

"What?"

"I—nothing," he decided, changing his mind about telling her. He wasn't ready to say that he, too, thought they would get along fine and that this marriage thing just might work.

But only if nobody hired a hit man, and only if he could find Ready Rita Warren.

Chapter Ten

"Sergeant Beltran?" He looked up from the paperwork he was trying to make disappear, and he was in no mood to be interrupted. Santos stood nervously in front of his desk.

"What is it, Santos?"

"That information you said you needed, Sergeant," she said, handing him a file. He hadn't asked for any files, and he was just about to tell her so in no uncertain terms. But her eyes shifted slightly to the right to where Burke stood listening.

He opened the folder and read quickly. "You're sure this is it?" he asked.

"Yes, Sergeant."

"Outstanding," he said.

He handed the file back to her. "No, wait," he said. "Let me keep that." Burke was entirely too interested in what he was doing, and Matt wasn't about to make it easy for him. "You let me know if this…changes."

"Yes, Sergeant." He went immediately back to his paperwork, but his mind was definitely on other things. Santos had done a good job. Quickly. Discreetly. She had been on hand the night he'd found Shorty in his car, and she had understood immediately that he needed to know whatever she could find out about Rita Warren's return. Santos knew more about his situation than anyone else on the post—except maybe for Burke. And, thanks to Burke, he'd had to have Santos call Corey on several occasions recently to let her know that his off-duty plans had abruptly changed. Burke had gotten his promotion after all, and one of the perks was that it was easier to give him hell. A whole lot easier.

But now Santos had brought him the exact address of where Rita Warren was supposed to be staying. He had no idea how she'd managed to come up with the information, and he didn't care how. He looked at the clock. It would be hours before he could check this out. He needed to talk to Rita before he could tell Corey that he was all hers. Thanks to Burke's penchant for sudden reassignments, he hadn't seen Corey in days. She probably thought he was trying to hide from her or something.

He managed to get away from Burke with just enough time to withdraw a significant amount of money from the bank before it closed, but it took him a while to find the right trailer park. He had never heard of it, and apparently it was one of those long-established sites everybody else in the world already knew about, hence the total absence of any kind of sign. Once he located the place, it took another major effort to locate the trailer. The residents were nothing if not closemouthed. He eventually had to come up with a significant bribe to get the information. It cost him twenty bucks to drive ten feet.

He parked behind a dented gray pickup truck, but he didn't get out. He sat in the car and waited. Somebody was definitely at home. He saw the curtains move. Rita would know immediately who he was—if she was here.

The front door finally opened and a soldier came out. He was barefooted and shirtless and wearing jeans instead of fatigues, but his haircut and his anxious look gave him away, the old is-this-official-or-is-this-going-to-get-me-shot look. Matt could both smell and see the beer buzz when the man bent to peer into the car.

"Tell Rita I want to talk to her," Matt said. It was by no means a request.

"Sergeant, I don't want any trouble—"

"Then tell her," he said.

"I don't think she—" He stopped and sighed. Resting directly between the rock and the hard place didn't seem to be to his liking, beer buzz or not.

"I owe her some money," Matt said. "Child support."

The soldier frowned. Clearly, this was the first he'd heard about a kid.

"I'll tell her," he said.

Matt didn't have to wait long. Rita came out almost immediately. He reached across and opened the car door on the passenger side, and she stood uncertainly for a moment before she got in. She was still pretty. She was trim and muscular from all the dancing, and she still had her big runway hair. But wherever she'd been the past few months, it wasn't some kind of health spa.

"Hey, Matt," she said, smiling broadly. "How's it going?"

"Just fine," he said without returning the smile. "Better than fine."

She took a lot of time getting situated in the bucket seat, and then she sat and jiggled one knee while she inspected the inside of the car.

"Looking for somebody?" he asked, and she flushed.

"No, I—"

"Aren't you even going to ask how she is or where she is?"

"No—well, yes. She's okay, right? I knew you'd take care of her."

"Who's the boyfriend?"

"Oh. That's Bugs. He's Airborne—like you. He's a great guy."

She glanced at him then. For affirmation of Bug's greatness, he supposed.

"He said you...had some money for me."

"I said that to get you out here."

"Oh," she said again.

"I understand you're looking to get the baby back," he said.

"Well, yes. She *is* mine. I love her. I really do." She tried smiling again. It wasn't nearly as easy as it had been before.

He didn't say anything. Maybe she did love

Shorty—insomuch as she was able. But he was beginning to think that the key to this parent thing was loving *more* than you were able.

"I've got an appointment with a lawyer and everything," she said.

"So Bugs is looking to be a daddy?"

"Bugs?" she said, as if she couldn't comprehend the question.

"Yeah. Bugs. The really great Airborne guy with the beer buzz you're living with."

"You're being mean to me, Matt. Why are you being mean to me?"

He held up both hands. "I'm just here to see if I can help you get the baby back, that's all."

She looked at him with some alarm. Regardless of what she might have told Lou, she didn't seem in any rush to return to the hallowed halls of motherhood.

"I thought maybe I could help pay for the lawyer. Something like that."

She smiled again. "Yeah. That would be good. You could help pay."

"So do you want to tell the lawyer to send the bill to me?"

She didn't say anything. He could almost see the wheels turning in her mind.

"I don't know if he would do that," she said finally.

"Well, then, how about if I just give the money to you?"

She had to stop herself from beaming. "Oh. Well, I guess that would work."

"So how much do you think it would cost?"

"Oh…gosh. Maybe a couple hundred?"

"That much?"

"Well, yes. These things aren't cheap, you know."

"No, I don't suppose they are. If I was to give you that much, you *would* give it to the lawyer," he said.

"Yeah, sure, I would. What do you take me for anyway?"

He looked at her. *You don't want to ask me a question like that,* he thought.

"Things do come up," he said. "I mean, you never know what the money might have to go for, right?"

"Right," she said, frowning. Clearly, she wasn't quite sure if she should agree with him or not.

He looked up at the sound of a door. Bugs had come outside to sit on the front steps, beer in hand.

"So are you going to give me the two hundred?" she asked.

"No." He reached into his breast pocket. "I'm thinking you might need…more than that."

"More?" she said, watching him take the bank envelope out.

"To do the best thing for your daughter. That is what this is all about, right? Doing the best thing for *her.*"

"Absolutely," she said.

"You know she's in a good home now," he said.

She tore her eyes away from the envelope. "Is she?"

"She's happy."

"Oh, that's good."

"I want her to stay happy."

"Well, yes. Me, too. I—"

She suddenly realized what he meant.

"How much money is in there?" she asked.

"More than you'd know what to do with."

"For the lawyer?"

"For making sure the baby stays happy, Rita."

She let her eyes meet his.

"No problem," she said, snatching the envelope out of his hand.

"Are you out of your mind?"

"You know, I wish people would stop asking me that," Corey said.

"Maybe the frequency should suggest something to you," Lou said, coming into the kitchen. "Are you baking something?"

"Brownies," Corey answered.

"Well, don't let them get done while I'm here. I'm on a diet."

"I'll do my best," she said.

She moved to the doorway to check on Shorty, who was still happily eating her afternoon apple while she watched her favorite children's video.

"I guess you know Beltran nearly had to call somebody to come revive me," Lou said when Corey came back into the kitchen. "He just walked into my office—right off the transport from the look of him and smelling like a wet dog—and boom! 'Corey Madsen and I are thinking about getting married and what do I do to petition for custody of Shorty?' I have never been so shocked in my life. You have no idea of the array of conflicting emotions

you two have put me through. I know him well
enough to halfway believe what he tells me, and I
know you well enough to think you would never—
and I mean *never*—marry somebody like him.''

Corey sighed. ''Why not? Why wouldn't I?''

''Corey, Goody Two-shoes does *not* marry the Big
Bad Wolf.''

''I think you mean Little Red Riding Hood.''

''I *mean* you and Matt Beltran! For God's sake,
what are you thinking!''

''I'm thinking about Shorty.''

''Corey, he is nothing like Jacob. When did Jacob
ever go bar-hopping on the Boulevard and then show
up with an illegitimate child? Besides that, the man
is career army—he's never going to be around when
you need him.''

''Neither was Jacob.''

''Yes, but he wasn't on the other side of the world.
I don't think Beltran has ever had any personal re-
sponsibilities in his life. As far as I know, he's never
even had a family.''

''Yes, he has. They just didn't happen to be blood
related. And he's a man at least inclined to do the
right thing—which a lot of men aren't, as you and I
both know—*and* he loves his daughter.''

''Does he happen to love you, too, while he's at
it?''

''It wouldn't be that kind of marriage.''

''Yes, and that's what worries me. You and Jacob
loved each other. How can you even think of settling
for anything less than that?''

''Don't you see? I've already been married to the
love of my life. No one can take Jacob's place. This

marriage would be for an entirely different reason, but that doesn't mean it can't work, or that it's any less of a marriage.''

''Does Matt understand he's getting short-changed?''

''I've been entirely truthful,'' Corey said. ''I'm going to make a home for the three of us. He's never had a real home. He isn't going to be short-changed.''

''If he's going to have to live in Jacob's shadow, he is. Believe me, he wouldn't like that. Matt Beltran is a proud man—or haven't you noticed?''

''I've noticed,'' she said, thinking of the night he had unceremoniously rejected her efforts to take him to bed.

''So you've absolutely made up your mind?''

She smiled. ''You mean the one I'm apparently out of?''

''Yes,'' Lou said. ''That one.''

''I've made up my mind. Now all I have to do is wait for Matt to make up his.''

''Well, then…I don't know what else to say. If there *is* a wedding, am I invited?''

''If you promise not to picket the ceremony.''

Lou laughed. ''So what does your family say about all this?''

''Quite a bit, actually.''

''Have they met the possible groom?''

''No.''

''But they're going to,'' Lou said. ''Before this thing is a done deal, I mean.''

''Why? Do you think they can talk *him* out of it?''

''Somebody needs to talk to somebody.''

"Lou, I know what I'm doing."

"Maybe. Maybe not. I think you're getting in way over your head here. A small piece of advice, Corey. He's not Jacob, and I think there'll be people standing in line to make sure he understands that. You're going to have to watch out for him. He may not know how to play the how-dare-you-marry-our-Corey game. He's liable to say exactly what he thinks—delivered with some good old military anathemas those people never even heard of."

Corey smiled. "You really like him, don't you?"

"That hardheaded son of a gun? I have been mad enough at him to punch him right in the nose—several times—but, yeah, I like him. I like you, too. But this is not what I foresaw when I called you that night to come get an abandoned baby."

It wasn't what Corey had seen either.

"You're totally against our getting married, then?" Corey said. "Is that what you're going to put in your report?"

"No. Actually, I'm not against it. I think staying here with you permanently—and with Matt when he's able to make it—would be a good thing for Shorty. I just have certain misgivings about whether or not Matt can take the heat of being a new parent *and* a new husband."

"Nobody can know that up front—about anyone."

"True. So I'm trying to keep an open mind here. Stranger things have happened, I guess—but damned if I know what they are. Oh, I did want to tell you something about Rita. She didn't keep her appointment with the lawyer. I have no idea why. Could be anything from no transportation to cold feet—or she may have flown the coop again. Corey—'' Lou abruptly stopped, then cautiously continued, ''Corey—''

''What, Lou? Go ahead and say it.''

''A marriage doesn't guarantee Matt will get custody of Shorty. You understand that, don't you? I can make my recommendation, but it's not a guarantee.''

''Yes, of course, I understand.''

''What are you going to do if you marry him for the baby's sake and then you can't get custody?''

''I'll worry about that when and if the time comes,'' she said.

''Corey—''

''Lou, please! I know what I'm doing.''

''So you keep saying,'' Lou said. ''I certainly hope so. Especially since this situation is entirely my fault.''

''It's not your fault. If it's anybody's fault, it's Rita Warren's.''

''I just—''

''Lou! Enough already!''

Lou smiled and shook her head. ''Okay. If you say you know what you're doing, then you do.'' She sighed. ''I...guess. So it's all up to Matt now?''

''Yes.''

''You think he's going to agree to the marriage?''

''Do you?'' Corey countered. ''You talked to him last.''

''Honey, all I know is what my mama used to tell me. 'Be careful what you wish for, because you just might get it.'''

They both turned around at the sound of a car

stopping out front. Corey recognized it immediately, and so did Shorty. She came running in from the den, abandoning the purple dinosaur and his friends for the soldier in the Corvette.

"You know, that's what I wanted for him," Lou said, watching Shorty do her little dance of anticipation by the front door. "I wanted him bonded with that child. Corey, I don't want to regret it."

They looked at each other. There was nothing Corey could say.

Matt stepped onto the porch. "Hey, Short Stuff," he said, bending down to see her through the door. "What are you up to?"

"Taking the door off the hinges if I don't hurry up and let you in," Lou said, holding on to the back of Shorty's T-shirt while she opened the door for him. "Corey, I'll see you later. You think about what I said. And you, too," she added to Matt, who didn't seem surprised by the admonishment. Corey supposed that Lou had given him all the pros and cons of their situation, as well. Or simply the "cons." Clearly, Lou didn't think there were all that many "pros."

But Corey didn't want to think about any of it. Her mind was made up; she had done all the thinking she intended to do. She had spent a long time sitting in the dark trying to summon some remnant of Jacob before she reached her decision. She couldn't do it. All those weeks after he died, it had been as if he had just left the room. She could still *feel* him near her. But he was gone now—for whatever reason— and there was simply no point in going over and over a problem that had only one solution.

The kitchen timer went off, and she went to get the brownies out of the oven. In the process she realized that Matt had come with her as far as the doorway. He stood there, with Shorty wrapped around his knees.

He looked so tired, and she had to suppress the impulse to ask him about it. She noted with some dismay how glad she was to see him. She had been glad to see him for some time now, regardless of how little she actually knew about him or how little they had in common. He was a complete enigma to her, one she felt compelled to unravel. He lived a life she couldn't even begin to imagine. It was his job to go in harm's way, one he himself had chosen. And she had no doubt that he was every bit as dedicated to his profession as Jacob had been to his.

For a moment she almost wished that the impression she had given her family was true, that some kind of wonderful love story between her and this man was about to unfold. She had been very careful not to suggest to her mother—from whom she had gotten her own heightened ability to discern ulterior motives—that this possible marriage to Mateo Beltran was anything less than a love match. She hadn't gone so far as to say that she couldn't live without him, but she hadn't quite told the truth, either. She did say that she respected him, appreciated his effort to do right by his child, and she indicated that, because of the circumstances, she would have to be the one who did the proposing. She just conveniently omitted the details about Rita Warren's sudden return and her own conviction that she simply couldn't cope with the loss of another person she loved. She hadn't been able to do anything about losing Jacob, but she could at least try to do something about Shorty.

Matt bent and picked up the baby. His eyes met hers when he straightened again. No matter how much she wanted—needed—to pretend that a marriage of convenience was all she required of him and that Shorty was the only consideration, it wasn't true. He wasn't simply a means to an end—no matter how hard she tried to convince herself otherwise.

The telephone rang, and she went to answer it. She recognized the voice on the other end of the line immediately.

"Corey, I want to talk to you," Jacob's mother said without prelude.

Corey held the receiver away for a moment, bracing herself for what could only be another ordeal.

"How are you, Evangeline?" she said with a cheerfulness she didn't begin to feel.

"I'm terrible. Corey, I need to talk to you. Right now."

"Now really isn't a good time, Evangeline—"

"Is *he* there?"

Corey glanced at Matt, who was obviously listening.

"You want me to go?" he asked.

"Yes," she said to Jacob's mother. "No," she said to him.

"Which is it?" he asked.

She covered the receiver with her hand. "I don't want you to go."

"Corey?" Mrs. Madsen said. "My husband and I are coming over. We'll see you in a little while."

"Evangeline, wait—" she began, but Mrs. Madsen had already hung up. "Oh, great," she said under her breath.

"What's wrong?" he asked, trying to put Shorty down. She held on to the neck of his T-shirt for dear life and refused to let her feet touch the floor. He lifted her up again.

"Jacob's mother and father are coming to talk to me."

"About what?" he asked, tickling Shorty, who was still hanging on.

"You know about what," she said.

"You mean there's going to be some kind of big family-crisis discussion thing?"

"Only if you've decided to marry me," she said, meeting his eyes.

She thought he was going to let the golden opportunity she had given him to declare his intentions pass him by.

"Is the offer still good?" he asked after a moment.

"I'm afraid so."

"Well, then, I guess you're in for it. I've thought about it, and I want to do the best I can for Shorty. So your terms are...acceptable."

They stared at each other, and she realized suddenly that she had been holding her breath.

"Is that a...yes?"

"Affirmative, Madsen."

"Oh. Well—" She swallowed heavily, hoping she didn't look like the trainee about to get shoved out the jump door again. "Good."

"So when do you want to do this?"

"I don't know—as soon as possible, I guess."

"Do you do want me to go now—before the Madsens get here?"

"You wish," she said, and he laughed. "Are you…going to stay?"

"Yeah, I'll hang around," he said. "No problem."

"It may get unpleasant."

He shrugged. "I'm a complete stranger about to walk off with their late son's wife. I wouldn't expect them to be happy about it."

He was looking into her eyes when he said it. His candor still surprised her. He wasn't given to personal revelations, but he did have a penchant for not sugar-coating the truth.

"Could you wash the apple off Shorty's face?" she asked suddenly.

He looked at his daughter. "What?" he asked in mock surprise. "You've got an apple face? Let me see. Last time I was here, you had a spaghetti face." Shorty grinned around the fingers she had stuck in her mouth.

"Matt?" Corey said as he turned to take Shorty down the hall to the bathroom.

"What?"

"*I'm*…happy about it," she said.

He looked at her for a moment, then nodded. He was surprised by the remark, she could tell, just as she could tell that he was…pleased.

But he didn't want her to know it.

"You heard the woman," he said to Shorty, pretending to noisily bite her cheek as he carried her down the hall. "Get the apple off the face. Come on, Golden Delicious—"

Corey stood still for a moment, then began moving around the room, straightening things that didn't need straightening.

I can't believe it, she kept thinking. *He's really going to do it.*

She closed her eyes at the thought of telling the Madsens. They were never going to understand, and she couldn't explain it.

When Matt and Shorty returned, the baby's face was shining clean and her hair had been brushed.

"Perfect," she said, smiling.

"See there?" he said to the baby. "We did good."

A car passed outside and Corey went to the window to look out. It was a false alarm.

"Car!" Shorty announced, and Corey smiled at her. She tried not to wring her hands.

"You're a big girl now, Madsen," he said. "You can do whatever you want—for whatever reason you want to do it. Can't you?"

"You'd think so," she said absently, still listening for vehicles.

She looked out the window again at the sound of another car. But it wasn't the Madsens. The Donahue family sedan was pulling into the driveway.

"Oh, no," she said.

"What?" he asked, trying to see.

"My mother and father are here," she said.

"Well—the more the merrier, I guess."

"You don't understand. This is *not* good."

"Why not? We'll just get the big announcement over with all at one time."

"They don't like each other. A lot."

"Who?"

"The Madsens and my parents. Somebody is going to say the wrong thing and then voices will be raised, my mother will cry, my father will walk out of the house and everybody will expect *me* to fix it."

He was frowning.

"You didn't think my life was like Beaver Cleaver's, did you?"

"Yes," he said.

"Oh, no, they're getting out—"

"Well, they would, wouldn't they? Take it easy, will you? I'm the one in the crosshairs here."

She wasn't the least bit reassured.

"Don't you think I should maybe know their names?" he asked.

Two car doors slammed in rapid succession.

"Hurry," he suggested.

"Sid and Billie Donahue," she whispered as her parents stepped onto the porch.

"He's Sid, she's Billie?"

"Right," she said, reaching for Shorty.

He wouldn't hand her over. "No way," he said. "You go find your own Barney T-shirt to hide behind. This one is *mine*."

"You don't need to hide. You're the one who jumps out of airplanes."

"Believe me, *that* is a whole lot easier than this."

But easy or not, he was the one who took charge and answered the door.

"Mr. and Mrs. Donahue," he said, giving Corey a wink. "I'm Matt Beltran. It's a pleasure to meet you." He held the door open with one foot while he shook hands with them both.

"And there's our beautiful Shorty," Corey's

mother said, kissing the baby's outstretched hand and giving some indication of how widespread Buck Rafferty's nickname had become. "She looks just like you, Matt," she insisted.

"No, ma'am," he said. "She's a lot prettier than I am."

Both her mother and father laughed.

So far, so good, Corey thought. Matt must have thought so, too, because he set Shorty down to toddle.

"We just thought we'd drop by and see how you're doing," her mother said.

"Did not," her father announced. "We heard Evangeline Madsen was coming over to give you hell about the sergeant here, and your mama said we had to hurry on over and make sure she didn't sneak up on you."

"Sid!" her mother said. "Honestly!"

"Well, it's the truth. Did you know the barbarians were about to storm the gates, son?" he asked Matt.

"Sir, yes, sir. I did."

"And you're still here? Good for you. See?" he said to Mrs. Donahue. "We rushed over here for nothing. They know all about it."

"How did *you* find out?" Corey asked.

"Big announcement at the beauty shop," Mr. Donahue said. "Your mother has spies all over the place."

"Sid!" Corey's mother said again. "You're going to have Matt thinking we're some kind of lunatics."

"If the shoe fits," he said, grinning at Matt.

They all looked around at the sound of another car.

"Second wave," Corey's father said as the Madsens parked next to the curb. "You ready, son?"

"Hoo-ah," Matt said.

Corey took a deep breath and went to let the Madsens in. She could see a very interested Buck standing on his front porch. She didn't blame him. Anybody who recognized all these cars and knew anything at all about her current situation would find these latest developments worth following.

She stood and waited for the Madsens to get out of the car, smiling if it killed her.

"Hi," she called to them.

"We were in the neighborhood," Mrs. Madsen said as she stepped up on the porch. "I see you have…company." She was *not* returning Corey's smile.

"Oh, not really," Corey said. "Just Mom and Dad. And Matt," she added because she realized that he had come to stand behind her. "Jake and Evangeline Madsen, this is Mateo Beltran."

Mrs. Madsen made no attempt to be polite. She brushed past Matt's outstretched hand without acknowledging it.

"Evangeline—" Jake Madsen said, hurrying inside after her.

"Well, this is not going well," Corey heard her father tell her mother.

"I knew it," her mother said.

Corey followed the Madsens into the house. There was no point in dragging this out. Evangeline stood in the room as if she was uncertain how she had gotten there.

"I'm glad you're all here," Corey said. "This is

a good time for me to tell you something." Shorty was pulling on her skirt, and she reached down to pick her up. The baby immediately laid her head on Corey's shoulder.

"I'm getting married," she said, looking directly at Evangeline. "To Matt," she continued, ignoring Evangeline's sharp intake of breath.

"Corey, you don't even know him," Evangeline said tearfully. "You're still in mourning. He had no right to ask you. You're not yourself or you wouldn't even consider—"

"He didn't ask me," she interrupted. "I asked him. And he's agreed to do it. We *are* getting married, and I want everybody to understand something. I love you all, but this is my personal business and it's not up for discussion. Sergeant Mateo Beltran is going to be my husband and I don't want anybody giving him a hard time. And that's all I have to say about it."

She turned and carried Shorty into the kitchen. She put the baby into her high chair and gave her some paper cups to unstack.

Goody Two-shoes and the Big Bad Wolf, she thought. The banns were posted. There was no turning back now.

She opened a cabinet and took down the first plastic container she could find, and she began tossing brownies into it, not realizing that Matt had followed her. But she didn't say anything to him and she didn't stop.

"Madsen," he said after a moment. "Madsen," he said again when she didn't look at him.

"What is it? Don't you like being talked about as if you're not even in the room?"

"I'm not crazy about it."

She looked at him finally. His face told her nothing when, as usual, she wanted to know everything there was to know.

Everything.

"If the three of us are going to be a family, then we're going to be a real family," she said abruptly. "We have to stick together—for Shorty's sake, if nothing else. I don't want anybody thinking this is just a whim. Jacob is dead, and I can't—" She stopped because her mouth had begun to tremble.

She tried to put another brownie into the container and missed. He came closer and caught her hand before she could pick it up again. His fingers were warm and strong around hers, and she clung to them. It was all she could do not to cry and all she could do not to make the same mistake she had made the other night and reach for him. He was so complex, so different from Jacob. And she wanted him in spite of it—or perhaps because of it. She didn't know anymore. She wanted to lie in his arms. She wanted to feel his hands and mouth on her body. He wouldn't be an easy lover, she knew that. He would recognize the longing and the need in her, and he would show her no mercy. He would take all she had to give, and she wanted him to. She had *loved* Jacob, loved him with all her heart. How could she be so—

"Take it easy," he said quietly.

She heard the front door slam, then two car doors, and then an engine start. She tried to smile and didn't quite make it.

"I really know how to clear a room, don't I?"

"Damn straight," he said.

The front door slammed again, and she sighed.

"Corey?" her mother said in the doorway. "We're going." She came in far enough to kiss the top of Shorty's head. "Be sweet, sugar pie," she said, kissing her again. "Matt, would you walk to the car with me? Corey, I'll tell your father goodbye for you."

Corey stood there. She had already understood that she wasn't to come along, but apparently her mother wasn't taking any chances.

People were leaving and the paper cups abruptly lost their fascination. Shorty began to fret, and Corey lifted her out of the high chair and carried her to the window where at least they could see the conversation between Matt and her mother. The two of them were standing on the sidewalk. Her mother was doing all the talking; Matt didn't seem to be saying much of anything. At one point, her mother reached out and took him by the hand.

And then she let go and walked the rest of the way to the car alone. Corey stepped out onto the porch so that Shorty could wave as the car backed out of the drive. She kept looking at Matt as he came up the walk. Whatever her mother had told him, he wasn't about to volunteer any information.

"What was that all about?" she asked in spite of his closed expression. "What did my mother say to you?"

She thought at first that he was going to give her one of his non-answers, but he didn't.

"She asked me to do something for you," he said.

"What?"

"She asked me not to marry you."

Corey didn't know what to say. She wasn't merely surprised that her mother had gotten in line behind Lou Kurian and Evangeline. She was astounded.

The phone rang and she gratefully went to answer it. It was Santos, urgently looking for Sergeant Beltran.

"It's for you," she said, holding the door open for him to come inside.

"Who is it?"

"Santos."

He frowned and made no attempt to meet her eyes. She stayed close enough to hear, but she couldn't tell anything from his side of the conversation. He hung up almost immediately.

"I have to go," he said.

He glanced at her, and this time the look held.

"I have to go," he said again. "I don't know how long this is going to take. I'll try to call you and let you know something. If I can't, I'll get Santos or somebody to do it for me."

She nodded.

"I'd...like to know if the marriage is still on or not," he said.

"It's on," she said without hesitation.

"You're sure?"

"Yes." The look of relief he gave her was more profound than anything he could have said.

She smiled. "I'm not playing here, Matt."

"No," he said. "I guess not."

"My mother doesn't know the details, but she

knows how guilty I'm feeling,'' she said, walking with him to the car.

"About Jacob."

She looked at him. "No. About you. I'm using you to take a child away from its mother, Matt. That's the bottom line."

"If I know the way things are between us and it's my choice as to whether or not I want to participate, how are you using me?"

"I can't keep Shorty any other way."

"Well, neither can I," he said. "We both have the same agenda here. But I...won't hold you to it, if you want out. I wouldn't blame you really. So far it's a no-go on getting anybody's blessing."

"Except for Buck and his lovely wife Carla, who are looking out the front window even as we speak,'' she said.

"Is that right?" He smiled slightly, more to himself than at her. She was beginning to recognize the expression. It was Sergeant Mateo Beltran, very pleased.

"See you, Short Stuff,'' he said to the baby, briefly catching the hand she was already waving at him. "Be a good girl."

But he still didn't leave. He stood there, looking into Corey's eyes.

I don't want you to go, she thought, but she didn't say anything, and neither did he. He abruptly got into his car and drove away.

Chapter Eleven

"How is it you are never the hell where you're supposed to be?" Burke asked.

Matt had no idea what the man was accusing him of, but he knew better than to even attempt to respond to it. He waited instead. Sooner or later he'd find out why Burke had tracked him down.

"The free ride is over," Burke said. "Maybe you got away with letting somebody else take your place on the tarmac that day. And maybe you *thought* you could get out of your overseas tour and hang around here humping the widow. But believe me, that's about to change. It has come to the attention of your commanding officer that your so-called family crisis situation is over."

Burke stopped, smiling slightly. The silence lengthened.

"I...don't know what you mean, Sergeant," Matt said finally.

"I mean we had a little visit from a certain night-club performer. This particular *artiste* was looking for you, but since you were over at the widow's and nobody wanted to come right out and tell her that but me, she had a conversation with the lieutenant instead. Let's just say what she told him and what he passed on to the captain was very...enlightening."

Burke paused again, clearly enjoying the game. When Matt didn't snap at the bait this time, his amusement faded.

"The compassionate leave you finagled has been canceled," Burke said. "For the next seventy-two hours you're going to be ass-deep in contingency planning. Getting all dressed up, you know what I mean? And I promise you, when that's done, you *will* have someplace to go. How does peacekeeping on the sunny, sandy shores of the River—"

Matt stopped listening. He concentrated on a spot just above Burke's head, his mind in turmoil. It took everything he had not to show it, and Burke knew it. He got through the briefing by sheer willpower alone and by clinging to a personal axiom that came, not just from his military experience, but from the early teachings of Father Andrew.

If a man insists on behaving like a horse's behind, my son, you just have to stand back and let him.

It had taken him fourteen years in the army to understand the true wisdom of the priest's advice.

Burke eventually wound down, but, as always, he wasn't past getting in a final shot.

"Beltran!" Burke called when Matt had been dismissed and was nearly out the door. "So sorry you won't be able to kiss the widow goodbye."

Matt ignored the gibe and went looking for Santos. He didn't have to look far. She and Meyerhauser were obviously waiting to find out how badly the you-know-what had hit the fan.

"How many of first squad are here?" he asked immediately.

"Jagger, McLachlan, Banba, George...and—"

"Kater," Meyerhauser supplied when Santos faltered.

"Round them up," Matt said.

"Now, Sergeant?" Meyerhauser asked.

"Yes," he said pointedly. "Now. And don't let Burke see you do it."

"Roger that," they both said.

Matt was impressed by how quickly the group assembled.

Teamwork was everything—he hoped. He had to wait until Burke was occupied, and it took him a few minutes before he could get to the small classroom where Santos had stashed them.

They all looked at him expectantly when he came in.

"Meyerhauser, you're on the door," he said.

"Hoo-ah," Meyerhauser said, taking his position and cracking the door just enough to be able to see down the hall.

"Okay, listen up," Matt said. "I've got a situation and I need some help—on a strictly volunteer basis." He stopped suddenly, not at all certain that he wanted to do this.

The silence grew awkward, but he still didn't say anything. He had no idea what Rita had told the lieutenant, and he couldn't waste time trying to find out and then trying to defend himself. It was absolutely imperative that he deal with the actualities. He was leaving the country in seventy-two hours and it was possible that he wouldn't come back. He had to take care of his daughter, and he couldn't afford to be embarrassed about what he needed done.

"What is it, Sergeant?" Santos said finally.

He looked at their faces and finally made up his mind.

"I...need you to get me married," he said.

His remark precipitated a scattered murmur of incredulous "hoo-ahs." Their attention had wandered slightly after the word "volunteer," but he had them all now, by God.

"I've got less than seventy-two hours to do it in. I'm not going to be able to get off the post for very long at a time—if at all. Somebody will have to coordinate my window of opportunity with getting Corey—my fiancée—down to the marriage license office, and then that has to be coordinated with the availability of a chaplain and one of the chapels here on the post. It's got to be timed down to the minute and it has to be done without Burke finding out about it."

"Are you sure Burke don't know nothing about this, Sergeant?" Meyerhauser asked from the door. "I mean, he ain't even got a clue?"

"No, he doesn't," Matt said. "And if this is handled right, he's not going to get one."

"How about Corey, Sergeant? Does she know?" Banba asked, and everybody laughed.

He smiled. "Sort of," he said. "She knows she's engaged, but she doesn't know I'm leaving to finish out my overseas tour. And I absolutely have to get married before I go." He realized suddenly how that sounded. They were all grinning.

"No, that is *not* the reason," he said. "Sometime in the next seventy-two hours will be my only chance for a long time. This won't be easy to pull off. If Burke gets wind of it, he's not going to be happy. I can take some of the heat for you, but then I won't be here. So, like I said, your involvement is strictly on a volunteer basis. I need to know if you're willing to give this thing a shot ASAP."

"I'm in, Sergeant," Meyerhauser said, still peeping through the crack in the door.

There was a chorus of "hoo-ahs" around the room.

"Okay, we need to get something on the table," Santos said to the group. "Then we'll get back to you, Sergeant."

"Good enough," he said, expecting that whatever details Santos knew about his situation with Shorty would go on the table, as well. "Too easy, right?"

"Hoo-ah!"

Corey was in the kitchen when two soldiers knocked at the back door. She recognized Santos immediately.

"Hi," she said, unlatching the screen and catching Shorty by the seat of her pants before she made a break for it. "Sergeant Beltran isn't here."

"Yes, ma'am, we know," Santos said. "We came to get you."

"Why? He's not hurt, is he?" Corey said, suddenly alarmed because they were both so serious and because she hadn't heard from Matt since he'd been called away.

"Oh, no, ma'am. We just don't have much time, is all. If you could hurry, that would be good. You've done everything on your checklist, right?"

"My...checklist?" She looked at the sheet of paper Santos was holding in her hand.

The two soldiers exchanged a look.

"You didn't call her?" Santos said to the other soldier.

"Me! That was Banba's—"

"Meyerhauser!"

"This is not my fault. Sergeant Beltran could have mentioned a *little* something to her, don't you think?"

"Now how was he supposed to do that with Burke hanging all over him—"

"Excuse me?" Corey said loudly. "I don't understand. What's going on? Where is it you want me to go?"

"Register of deeds—to get the marriage license," Santos said. "Right now."

"But—"

"We have to make sure you have in your possession every item on this list pertaining to your situation. We have to make sure you can answer correctly every question on this list pertaining to your situation. Understood?"

"Well...yes. That part I get."

Santos handed her the paper. "Excellent. I'll get the baby and turn off the burners and any appliances. Then I'm going to ride with you to the register's. Meyerhauser is going to stay here and advise the Raffertys where they need to go for Phase Two—"

"The Raffertys?"

"Yes, ma'am. Your wedding guests. Miss Lou is coming, too. We tried to get Mr. and Mrs. Donahue, but their neighbor said they'd gone to the beach for the rest of the week and we couldn't locate them, what with the critical time restraints. Please, ma'am. I really need you to move it."

Corey looked down at her paint-splattered jeans and her faded N.C. State T-shirt. "I can't go like this," she said. She didn't even have her shoes on.

"It's go like that or scrub the operation, ma'am. I mean it. You need to do this stuff on the list—like *yesterday*—and then we have got to go."

"Are you sure you have the right house?"

"Yes, ma'am. Hurry! Please!"

"All right, all right," Corey said, still somewhat bewildered. Clearly, a number of pages in the most recent chapter in her life had been edited without her input.

The list wasn't all that difficult. She had a current driver's license. She didn't have a recent divorce decree. She didn't know the answers to some of the questions, however—such as where the ceremony would take place and the name of the presiding minister. Fortunately, Santos did, and the most difficult stumbling block to their immediate departure became finding Corey's missing shoes.

"Shorty, have you carried off my shoes again?"

Corey said, getting down on her hands and knees to look under the furniture. "What did you do with them, baby?"

"Hurry, ma'am," Santos kept saying.

"Huh-wee," Shorty said, clapping her hands with excitement.

"I'm hurrying!" Corey said, finally locating her shoes in the wastepaper basket. She slipped them on as she grabbed her purse, the diaper bag and the car keys.

"Let's go, let's go!" the other soldier was yelling by the back door.

"I don't suppose I have time to—"

"No, ma'am, you do not," Santos assured her.

Corey sighed and picked up the baby. Surprisingly, Santos let Corey drive—but she didn't let her park.

"I'll take it from here, ma'am," Santos said. "You get Shorty and get in there."

"Santos, why are we doing this?"

She looked at Corey. "I thought you knew, ma'am. The sergeant is going to the Balkans."

"But he just came back."

"He didn't complete his tour, because of the baby being left in his car and everything."

"But that's still not settled."

"As far as the army is concerned, it is. Hurry, ma'am," Santos said again. "Sergeant Beltran wants this squad to get him married, and we're going to do it—if that's okay with you, of course."

Corey couldn't keep from smiling, because it was a little late for Santos to be consulting her. She took the baby out of the car seat, and she hurried as fast as she could while still carrying Shorty and her purse and the diaper bag. She had no idea where to go once she was inside, since she and Jacob hadn't gotten their license here. But like the rainy night she had gone to pick up an abandoned baby, someone had spotters out. She could hear a deep male voice calling her name when she was hardly inside the front doors.

"Corey Donahue Madsen!"

"Here!" she said.

"Outstanding, ma'am!" another one of Beltran's representatives said, taking her by the arm. "We need to—"

"I know," she said. "Hurry."

"Roger that. This way."

Her purse slid off her shoulder and then the diaper bag, but he didn't let her stop. Both accessories bumped along in between them, dangling from the crook in her arm.

"Is Sergeant Beltran here yet?" she asked, trying to keep up.

"No, ma'am."

"But he's coming, isn't he?"

"If Burke don't catch him," he said, making her turn left down a hallway.

"Who is Burke?"

"Bad news, ma'am. He ain't somebody you'd want at the wedding."

The wedding.

It was fairly apparent now that these military people actually thought she was getting married in the midst of all this craziness—that is, if she had any breath left to say "I do."

"Now what?" she asked when they reached the marriage license office.

"See that soldier up there near the front of the line?"

"The one waving?"

"Yes, ma'am, that one. He's saving a place for you and Sergeant Beltran. You go on up there where he is, and you might not want to mention too loud that he ain't actually the guy you're supposed to marry, okay?"

"Right," she said, moving forward with Shorty in her arms. "Have you ever?" she said as she wound her way to her assigned place, and Shorty vigorously shook her head no. "Me, either," Corey assured her.

"Here you go, ma'am," the next soldier—McLachlan—said, making room for her in the queue. "Let me take something for you, ma'am." The something turned out to be Shorty, who immediately took a liking to him. He held her as if he thought she might break, and kept looking at his watch.

"Is he late?" Corey asked, because she was in no way privy to the timetable—or anything else, for that matter.

"Not...very," McLachlan said.

"Enough to worry?"

"Well, we could get a little anxious about it," he admitted. "No, wait, I see him! Okay, ma'am. I'm going to step aside now—if you'd take *this*—"

He handed Shorty back to her. "Here you go," he said, but he was talking to Matt. "Too easy, Sergeant!"

"Good job," Matt said to him. "Santos is waiting out front."

"Roger that," the soldier said, hurrying away.

Corey felt infinitely better now that Matt was here, but she stood there awkwardly, not knowing quite what to say to him. She looked up at him, her eyes searching his, oblivious suddenly to the noise and confusion around them. She had thought he looked tired the last time she'd seen him. That situation clearly hadn't changed.

"How long have you got before you leave?" she asked.

"I'm leaving tomorrow—early," he said.

"It's…dangerous, isn't it? Where you're going."

He looked away. "Crossing the street is dangerous, Madsen. Hey, baby girl," he said abruptly to Shorty, and she reached for him. He took her out of Corey's arms.

"You aren't supposed to be here, are you?" Corey said.

"We're not going to worry about that now, okay? We've got to go with first things first."

They moved up in the line. If anyone had noticed that she'd changed potential soldier husbands, nobody commented on it. She stood there, trying to do what he said and not worry, but the list was growing ever longer by the minute. She could feel Matt looking at her, and she was all too conscious of the fact that she was wearing her porch-painting clothes. She had planned to touch up the latticework this afternoon, not walk down the aisle. She didn't have on any makeup; and her once-neatly-pinned-up hair was all coming down. At one point he reached to tuck a long strand that was hanging in her face gently behind her ear. She looked into his eyes again. Maybe

Lou was right. Maybe he was being short-changed. He deserved better than he was getting. He deserved a lot better.

"You okay with this?" he asked.

"Are you?" she countered.

"Yeah, I'm fine."

"Are you still going to be fine when you're in jail for running off to the courthouse?"

He smiled instead of answering. "I tried to get your mom and dad."

"I know. Santos told me. Who is Burke?" it suddenly occurred to her to ask.

"He's the newly promoted Sergeant First Class."

"You're not one of his favorite people, I take it."

"You could say that."

"You really think he'd try to keep you from getting married?"

"Only if he knew about it."

Suddenly he was looking at her so intently.

"What?" she asked.

"I...didn't think you'd be here."

She laughed. "I don't think Santos and Meyerhauser considered that up for discussion."

"They're good soldiers. See the hill, take the hill," he said.

"Next!" the clerk yelled, and things progressed rapidly from there. Santos's list had been beyond exact.

"I tell you what," the clerk said. "If everybody came in here this prepared, I'd think I'd died and gone to heaven. You all come back again—anytime."

"No, thanks," Matt said. "This is it."

"Now what?" Corey asked as they walked quickly outside.

"Santos is going to get you to the church on time," he said.

"Yes, I really look like I'm ready to get to the church."

"You look...fine," he said, and she grinned.

"Tactful to a fault, aren't you, Beltran?"

"No, I don't think I've ever been accused of that," he said, smiling in that mischievous-little-boy way he sometimes had.

"Where will you be while I'm getting to the church?" she asked.

"I have to put in an appearance so Burke doesn't miss me—and then I'll come there."

"Are you sure?"

"No," he said, handing her Shorty and the license. "But I'm going to give it my best shot."

A pickup truck screeched to a halt at the curb in front of them, the door already open, and Matt barely made it inside before it took off again.

"Bye-bye," Shorty said belatedly to her rapidly disappearing father.

"Okay, baby girl," Corey said. "Now we're ready for Phase Two—whatever that is." Santos appeared in the Volvo as if on cue, and Corey's departure from the courthouse was considerably less dramatic than Matt's had been. They drove to Bragg Boulevard, then headed back in the direction they'd come.

"How much of a chance have we got?" Corey asked at one point.

"Ma'am?"

"Of pulling this wedding off. How much of a chance?"

"I'd say...fifty-fifty."

Corey took a deep breath and looked out the window.

"No, fifty-fifty is good," Santos said. "At first it was a one in ninety-nine chance. Well, actually, it was zero in a hundred. But look how far we've gotten. We've got the license. Meyerhauser and McLachlan have gone to get the chaplain. The Raffertys and Miss Lou should already be there. And if Sergeant Beltran can give us just five good minutes, this thing is a done deal."

"And if he can't?"

"Well, then, we'll just have to figure out a way to get you and him to Vicenza at the same time."

"Italy?"

"Affirmative, ma'am. To tell you the truth," she said, making a right turn, "it couldn't be much harder than getting you and him synchronized down at the courthouse."

Corey could see the chapel from the Boulevard, but it took a number of turns to actually get there. Lou was waiting out front. Corey got Shorty out of the Volvo and walked in her direction. Lou was grinning from ear to ear.

"Nice dress," Lou teased, coming to greet her.

"Oh, please," Corey said. "I'm just lucky I wasn't in the shower."

Lou kept staring at her.

"What!" Corey said in exasperation. "I know I look awful."

"No. You look...happy. A little worried maybe—but happy."

Corey dismissed the observation with a flick of her hand.

"No, I mean it. Are you sure this isn't going to be 'that kind of marriage' after all?"

"I'm not sure about anything," Corey said. "I have no idea if the groom is even going to make it to the ceremony. All I know is Rita wants Shorty back and Matt is leaving for the Balkans tomorrow."

"Corey—"

"Don't start," she said, holding up one hand.

"You know it's not too late to change your mind," Lou said anyway.

"I don't want to change my mind," she said, holding Shorty close for a moment. She glanced at Lou. Lou was smiling. "What!"

"Nothing. Here comes Santos with your stuff. You wouldn't happen to have a hairbrush and some lipstick in either of those bags, would you?"

"I don't carry hairbrushes and lipstick. I carry diapers and cereal," she said.

But she did have a piece of a comb. She hunted for it while Santos took Shorty for a walk under the pine trees. She hastily took the pins out of her hair and began to try to rake out the tangles.

"Did you know Matt tried to get my parents here?" she asked.

"Yes," Lou said.

"My mother asked him to his face not to marry me, and he still tried to get them here."

"Well, that's the kind of man he is. Wait a minute—you missed a sprig,'' she said as Corey worked to do something positive with her hair.

Another car arrived. The Raffertys. And then two pickup trucks. The chaplain—a pleasant-looking, slightly balding man—and a number of Matt's squad.

Corey took a deep breath. No Beltran.

Santos picked up the baby and walked back toward the chapel, intercepting the chaplain on his way in—to give him the latest update, Corey supposed. He listened intently to whatever Santos said to him, then nodded. A few of the squad members went on into the chapel.

''Ma'am,'' they said to her as they filed by. Two of them were harmonizing on ''Chapel of Love.''

She smiled, and she stood and waited for the Raffertys. She saw immediately that Carla was all teary-eyed and Buck was beaming.

''I hope I haven't brought you out here for nothing,'' Corey said, hugging them both.

''You don't worry about a thing, Corey. Matt will be here,'' Buck said.

She forced herself to smile, wanting desperately to believe it.

''We love you,'' Carla said. ''And we're so happy to be here. We think what you and Matt are doing is just...wonderful. Buck's got the camera and if he can remember to take the lens cap off, you're going to have plenty of pictures.''

''Now, Mother, when did I ever forget the lens cap?''

''The Grand Canyon,'' she said.

''Besides that.''

''Niagara Falls.''

Buck grinned. "I better quit while I'm behind," he said, taking his wife's arm. "We'll see you inside, honey."

The chaplain walked up. "Corey," he said, introducing himself and shaking her hand. "I've heard a lot about you."

"I...wish I could say the same," she said.

He chuckled. "Yes, well, today is a bit unusual, isn't it? Matt said you had been left out of the loop, so to speak." He looked at his watch. "Time over target—oh, minus ten, I'd say," he said. "I need to ask you a few questions. Will you come inside now?"

"No, I think I'd rather wait for him out here." *Where I can make a break for it if he doesn't show.*

He smiled again and nodded. "Fine," he said, thumbing through the small book he carried.

"I can take the baby on inside," Santos said. "Did I hear you say you had cereal?" Corey got the small plastic bag full of cereal from her purse. "There's a juice box in the diaper bag," she said. Shorty was immediately interested and went with Santos happily.

Corey answered all the chaplain's questions, and she realized after a moment that he intended to stay out here and wait with her.

Minus ten came and went. Corey began to pace. Santos came back outside to pace with her.

"Buck and Carla are looking after Shorty," she said. "She's just about asleep."

Corey nodded, looking around sharply at the sound of another vehicle. It went on past. She sighed and walked a little distance away to the pine trees, not realizing that Santos had come with her.

"If he's not here, it's because Burke has him hung up somewhere," Santos said quietly.

Corey didn't say anything. They stood for a time in silence.

"Ma'am," Santos said, and Corey looked at her. "There he is."

Corey looked around. Beltran was approaching at a run from a nearby parking lot. She walked out to meet him.

"Let's go, Madsen," he said, catching her by the hand. "Not much time."

"Matt—"

"Later," he said, pulling her along with him to where the chaplain stood.

"If I understand the plan here, there isn't going to be a later—"

"Sure there will—but it may take a few months. You haven't changed your mind, have you?"

"No, *I* haven't—"

"Well, me, either. But we've got to hurry, okay? Sir, we've got to hurry, sir," he said to the chaplain.

"I can do that," he said.

They let the chaplain go in first, then they began to walk down the aisle, still holding hands. Their arrival was apparently unheralded, and there was a scramble among the guests to get to a pew.

"I'm sorry," Matt said.

"About what?"

"This is nothing like…what you had before."

She looked at him. "I don't think this is like what *anybody* had before, Sergeant."

He grinned. "Maybe not. Santos," he said abruptly when he saw her.

"Sergeant?"

"I need a best man."

"Who, Sergeant?" she asked, ready to go get him.

"You, soldier."

"*Me?*"

"You put this thing together, didn't you?"

"Yes, Sergeant."

"Well, then, you're the man."

"*Woman,* Sergeant," she said, smiling broadly.

"You got a bridesmaid, Madsen?" he asked.

"I think my bridesmaid is asleep," Corey said, looking to where Shorty lay draped over Buck's shoulder. Carla was enthusiastically taking pictures.

"Well, then, we'll just have to wing it," he said.

"What a novel concept," she said, smiling into his eyes.

The chaplain stood waiting. "Will you be exchanging rings?"

"No," Corey said.

"Yes," Matt corrected.

"I don't have a ring," she said.

"Well, I do—don't I?" he asked Santos.

"Affirmative," she said, getting it out of her pocket and showing it to the chaplain.

"Let's go, sir," Matt said.

"Dearly beloved—"

"Sir, I don't think we have time for all that, sir," he said.

"Oh—well. Let's move along then. If you will join hands—oh, you've already done that. In that case, Mateo Beltran, will you have this woman to be your lawfully wedded wife? Will you love her, comfort her, honor and keep her, in sickness and in health, forsaking all others, and keep you only unto her, so long as you both shall live?''

''I will,'' he said, looking at Corey. She noted for the first time that the hand that held hers was trembling slightly.

''And Corey Donahue Madsen, will you have this man to be your lawfully wedded husband? Will you love him, comfort him, honor and keep him, in sickness and in health, forsaking all others, and keep you only unto him, so long as you both shall live?''

''I will,'' she said, still holding Matt's gaze.

''And both of you—will you have each other for better or worse, richer or poorer, in sickness and in health, to love and to cherish, until death do you part?''

''I will,'' they said in unison.

''The ring, please.''

It took a bit of fumbling on Santos's part to get it.

''Mateo, repeat after me...'' the chaplain began, but Matt didn't wait for him.

''Corey,'' he said, looking into her eyes. ''This ring is a token of my respect and it's a token of my promise to you—to be a good husband and to make a good life for you and for Shorty, and to do everything I can to make sure that you never regret taking this chance with me.'' He slipped the ring on her finger, a simple gold band that fit perfectly. ''I'll even behave,'' he whispered to her, making her smile. ''Okay, sir,'' he said to the chaplain.

''Forasmuch as Mateo and Corey have—''

''Sir, hurry, sir.''

The chaplain cleared his throat. ''Forasmuch as Mateo and Corey...in the presence of these here gathered…'' he began again, but then he abruptly concluded with, ''Inowpronounceyoumanandwife. You may kiss your bride.''

Matt kissed her chastely on the lips, drawing an immediate response from the squad, but Corey didn't hesitate. She stepped into his embrace and hugged him tightly.

''Thank you,'' she whispered against his ear.

''My pleasure,'' he said, returning her hug.

They turned to walk down the aisle.

''Wait, wait,'' the chaplain said. ''You need to sign this.''

''The new name?'' Corey asked when it was her turn.

''That's correct,'' the chaplain said.

She signed, and then she took Matt's arm to walk outside, standing with him while he accepted the well wishes of the soldiers who had brought all this about. She couldn't keep from smiling.

The bride was attired in paint-splattered jeans with peek-a-boo knees and she carried a black leather purse in lieu of the bridal bouquet…

She stepped away from him for a moment to see about Shorty, who was still asleep, but who had changed shoulders and now rested on Carla's.

''It was a beautiful ceremony, Corey, honey,'' Carla said. ''I'm going to just…*bawl.*''

''Mother, don't go blubbering and wake up that baby,'' Buck admonished. ''Come on over here. I think Matt wants to talk to us.''

''Corey,'' Lou said behind her. ''I honestly believe you're right.''

''About what?'' Corey asked.

"I don't think this is going to be any less of a marriage, regardless of the circumstances and the reason for it."

Corey smiled, looking around to where Matt stood deep in conversation with Carla and Buck. He caressed Shorty's head once, and then he reached into his pocket and gave Buck an envelope.

"He's giving Buck his letter," Lou said quietly.

Corey looked at her. "His letter? I don't understand."

"It's a soldier thing. He's asking Buck to give the letter to you if anything happens to him."

Corey stood there, watching a ritual she hadn't even known existed before today, the realization washing over her that this—right now—might be all the life with Matt Beltran she would ever have.

He shook Buck's hand, and then he said something to his squad, something that met with a resounding "Hoo-ah!"

Corey immediately walked to him, but that same pickup truck arrived, the one that had whisked him away from the courthouse. Once again it screeched to a halt, the passenger side door flung wide.

He kissed Shorty on top of her head, hugged Corey one last time, and then he was gone.

Chapter Twelve

The contingency meetings dragged on. It was the army way to have more Plan B's than it knew what to do with—which was why it was the best in the world.

Matt paid attention, but he had to work at it. He kept seeing Corey's face, kept marveling that she had gone through with the marriage no matter how bizarre things had gotten. And Shorty. She'd be almost two when he saw her again. She'd be a little person by then—and maybe she wouldn't even know who he was. Maybe neither one of them would know.

"Beltran!" one of the lieutenants said. "The captain's still looking for you."

Still? he thought on the way to find out the big "now what?" He expected the absolute worst, particularly with Burke lurking around. He finally located the captain in the hallway, but he had to wait until the man had signed all the pages on numerous clipboards.

He looked up at Matt, expecting something else that required his signature. "Oh," he said. "Beltran—here." He handed Matt a card.

Matt looked at it, then up at the captain. He didn't know what to say.

"You did get married this afternoon?" the captain said.

"Sir, yes, sir," he answered, because it was obvious that the captain already knew.

"Well, that's your...wedding present, I guess. Courtesy of Lou Kurian, with a few good words from Chaplain Bob—he was the second wave. Miss Lou twisted a lot of arms to get this—one of them was mine. It is amazing how that woman can get you to do something you don't want to do and make you think it's all your idea. She says I should tell you you owe her big-time."

Matt looked down at the card again.

"What?" the captain said. "You don't know what to do with a four-hour honeymoon? If that's the case, I could probably find somebody around here—"

He tried not to grin. "Sir, no, sir. I know what to do."

"Then I suggest you stop wasting time here talking to me. Dismissed."

Damn, Miss Lou, Matt kept thinking on his way out. He knew she had clout on the post, but this was on the high side of a miracle, even with a chaplain's help.

Since his car had been stored for the duration, he

had to call a taxi to get to Corey. Four hours, he kept thinking. Only two in actuality. But a lifetime compared to no time at all.

It had rained just enough to run the humidity off the scale. If the cab had an air conditioner, he couldn't tell it. At one point he rolled down the window, but it didn't help. Maybe Corey wouldn't be glad to see him, he thought as the driver turned onto her street. Maybe she was happy to have gotten rid of him as quickly as she did, and she wouldn't want him showing up again when he was supposed to be gone. There were no lights on in the front of the house when he arrived. He looked at his watch. Twenty-three hundred.

"You want me to wait?" the cabdriver asked.

"No," he said. He paid the man and got out, lugging his duffel bag with him. The night was heavy with the scent of pine trees and honeysuckle. Every house on the street was dark.

He stood on the sidewalk for a moment, then went around to the side porch to knock, because it was closer to her bedroom and because he thought he could see the small lamp on in the hall.

He didn't have to knock. She was awake. He could see her sitting in the semidarkness, and he thought that she must have been expecting him, because she came to him quickly, opening the door wide to let him come inside.

But she didn't say anything and neither did he.

There was no time for words. He reached for her, holding her tightly, reminding himself that he had to go slowly, that, married or not, he couldn't just come here and jump all over her. It was an entirely new sensation for him, to want *her* and no one else. Not *a* woman, but *the* woman. She must have been outside for a time before he arrived; he could smell the night air on her, feel that her cheeks were moist.

Or had she been crying?

He leaned back, trying to see, but she wouldn't let him look or ask. She lifted her mouth to his, and he completely lost his train of thought.

Hot, openmouthed kisses, her body straining against his. Giving. Taking.

Oh, God, Corey.

His hands were shaking, his knees weak with desire. She stepped away from him and took him by the hand, leading the way through the darkened house to the bedroom. Some part of him tried to mind that he would lie with her in Jacob's bed. Some part of him tried to remember how adamant he'd felt about not ever having her husband's ghost there between them. But at this moment, he didn't care about Jacob. Jacob was dead and gone. *He* was alive, and the only thing that mattered was being with her now for what little time he had left.

The bedside lamp was on, and the room was smaller than he expected. He thought that maybe this wasn't the room she had shared with Jacob after all. Maybe it was the room she'd had when she was a little girl and had stayed the night at her grandmother's house.

She sat on the edge of the bed, and he knelt in front of her. She put her hands in his. He wanted to look at her. He wanted to touch her and taste her. It was as if he hadn't really noticed the details, but now—*now*—he was seeing every beautiful part of

her. Her hands, small and lost in his. Her eyes—
hazel—searching his for something she desperately
needed and he was so afraid he didn't have.

He removed his hands from hers, lifting them to
cup her face and bring her mouth to his.

So sweet.

Corey.

Her lips parted, yielding just for him, giving him
more and more until his mind reeled from it.

So good!

She tasted so good. His arms slid around her waist
and he pressed his face into her lap, shaky and
breathless, the demands of his body driving him hard.
Never in his numerous fantasies about her did he
think it would be like this, that he would feel so
much, need so much.

He lifted his head to look at her, and she moved
to the middle of the bed, watching, waiting for him
to come to her. He hurried, cursing the fact that there
was no speedy way to get out of jump boots. And
he didn't hesitate. He wanted them both naked, and
he tumbled her backward, his body covering hers,
his hands sliding up under the sleep shirt she was
wearing. She didn't have anything on underneath it,
and she was so soft and smooth. How could she be
so…soft?

He pulled at the wide neck of the shirt, baring her
breast. He kissed her there, tasting, exploring with
lips and teeth and tongue, the scent of her body—
her scent—subtle and yet infinitely arousing, urging
him onward, fueling his desire until he ached with
it.

But the soft moan she gave as he suckled her compelled him to linger. He lost himself in the pleasure of discovery. She wanted him to touch her. She rose under his hands and his mouth, and he was only too happy to oblige.

The damn shirt was in the way. She helped him pull it over her head. His dog tags were in the way. He tore them off and let them fall.

There was nothing between them now.

No, hell, there was still one more thing.

"I don't—I'm not—prepared," he managed to say.

"It's okay," she said.

He didn't know what that meant exactly. He didn't care. His birth control mind-set completely left him at the sensation of her warm body sliding against his. All this time he had been so careful with her, so determined not to let himself get emotionally involved. He would want her, yes. Perhaps even have her, but always on his own terms and with the firm conviction that he could—and would—walk away.

But his worst nightmare had come true—and his impossible dream, a dream so precious and buried so deep that, given the opportunity, he would never have been able to put it into words. He'd been waiting all this time, without even realizing it, for her, for the one person who, just by being, could take the loneliness away.

"Corey," he said aloud, because her eyes were closed and he was desperate for her to see him. *Him.* Not a surrogate Jacob. He braced himself above her. Her face was stormy with desire.

"Corey..." he said again.

Her eyelids fluttered open, and her lips parted. She

reached upward, drawing him to her, giving a soft "oh" sound he felt more than heard when he entered her. She was so tight and hot around him. He tried to hold back and he couldn't.

She stared into his eyes, into his soul. He thrust deeply, loving her with his heart and his body and his mind.

Did she know? Did she?

Corey!

"How old are you?" she asked quietly. Her hand rested lightly on his chest. He had thought she was asleep, or perhaps he was the one who had been dozing, because the question made no sense to him.

She moved so that they were lying face-to-face. "I don't know how old you are," she said. "Tell me."

"It was on the marriage license."

"Who had time to look at the marriage license?" she said pointedly, and he laughed softly.

"I'm…thirty-two."

"And your birthday is…"

"September the twenty-first—or that's the official position."

"What does that mean?"

"It means I don't know for sure. Father Andrew picked the date—Saint Matthew's feast day—because my name was Mateo. I told you I couldn't remember a lot of things after the accident. The car we were riding in…burned. They found some papers in what was left of a suitcase—a piece of a birth certificate for me—but they couldn't read all of it.

Father Andrew thought it would be easier to just give me a birthday himself.''

"September twenty-first is good," she said.

"Well, I've never had a problem with it. But then, I've never been much for birthdays.''

She was looking into his eyes in that way she had, and he suddenly tightened his arms around her, pressing her close, burying his face in the fragrance of her hair. He could feel the time slipping away, and it was killing him.

"I don't want to talk anymore," she said, as if he had started the conversation.

"Neither do I," he said. He was afraid of talking. There were only two things for them to talk about— the sins and sorrows of the past or worry about the future, and he didn't want to deal with either one of them. He only wanted the now. He wanted to lose himself in her—before it was too late.

"Close your eyes," she whispered.

"Why?"

Her mouth lightly touched his, then withdrew when he sought more. "Because I'm going to sneak up on you," she said, still whispering, her knee sliding between his thighs.

"Why?" he asked again, smiling now, already aroused, already needing her again.

"So I can show you...so I can give you back—" Her hands moved downward to touch him, and his breath caught "—everything...you gave...me..."

He awoke with a start. He had to leave—now— before he said anything he had no right to say. He understood the perimeters. The marriage was for

Shorty. The sex was a very significant, incredible perk. And their lives were complicated enough without him burdening her with his personal revelations, particularly when—for the first time in his life—he had the shipping-out blues.

He had meant every single word of the "for better or worse" part of the marriage ceremony. No. He had meant every single word of it all, condensed though it might have been. And what the hell good was it going to do him? Corey didn't care about him in that way.

He kept looking at her, marveling at what a passionate woman she had turned out to be. She was sleeping now, her hair spread out on the pillow. He liked her hair. She was the only woman he'd ever really known with hair that color, a kind of dark, rich auburn that always made him want to put his hands into it. He wanted to now. He wanted to wake her up and—

He closed his eyes against the rush of feeling.

I love you, Corey.

How easy it would be to say and mean *those* words, too.

He got dressed as quietly as he could, then he walked through the house to the den where he'd left his duffel bag, opening it to get the small teddy bear out of it. The bear wore "cammies," a deliberate ploy on his part to remind his daughter of her absent father, even if she was too little to understand what was going on. He took it to the room where Shorty lay sleeping and put it where she would see it when she woke up. She loved stuffed animals almost as much as she loved kitten books and meat sticks.

He stood by the crib for a long time. If there was anything positive about this situation, it was that he was leaving his baby girl in good hands. He wouldn't have to worry about her as long as she was with Corey. He still didn't know what Rita's coming to the post to see him had been about. He didn't think it had been a deliberate attempt on her part to get him out of the way. *That* was Burke's doing. Burke must have done a real number on her, gotten her to believe that she'd been royally used and abused by bad old Sergeant Beltran, the same Sergeant Beltran who had sat and listened to her talk about her dreams of fame and fortune enough to know that a baby girl—no matter how much Rita loved her—just didn't figure anywhere in the big picture. And "love" didn't mean squat if it didn't translate into what was best for the kid.

He wanted to kiss Shorty goodbye, but he couldn't get to her without lowering the crib rail, and he didn't want to wake her. He reached in and took her tiny hand for a moment instead.

Then he went into the kitchen to telephone for a cab. He had to get out of here, and he had to get out now. He didn't plan to wake Corey, either. He would just go. It would be better—easier.

But she was standing in the doorway when he hung up the phone. She was wearing the sleep shirt again and she was barefoot, her hair all tumbled from their lovemaking. She looked…beautiful.

"Were you just going to leave and not say anything?" she asked. There was a slight quiver in her voice.

"Yes," he said evenly.

"No goodbyes, no nothing?"

"No."

"What did you do? Leave twenty bucks on the dresser?"

"Corey—"

"Did you by any chance leave an address lying around somewhere? Someplace where I could at least write to you?"

"I don't want you to write to me."

She came closer. "Why not?"

"Because I don't want you to."

She came closer still. "Why?" she asked again.

He didn't answer her.

"Why?" she asked one more time.

"Because I couldn't stand it if you did!" he said. "I've learned to get along without that kind of thing. It's how I survive. Mail call doesn't mean anything to me. I don't need it. I don't want to need it. I can't—" He stopped because she had come close enough to lean against him.

"Okay," she said, and he put his arms around her, holding her close.

"This is killing me," he said against her ear. "Do you understand?"

She nodded. "I don't want to make it worse for you, but you have to tell me so I—"

"Shh," he said. "Kiss me."

She lifted her mouth to his, clinging to him hard. He could feel her trembling.

"You're not going to cry, are you?"

"I want to," she said. "I want to really bad."

"Don't, okay? Kiss me again."

She did.

He heard a car at the curb. "Cab's here," he said, his voice husky and strange-sounding to him. "Walk me as far as the door." She did as he asked, but he still thought she might cry.

"Wait," she said when he bent to pick up his duffel bag. "I have something for you." She disappeared into the kitchen briefly. When she returned, she pressed a key—a house key—into his hand. "This is for when you get back, so you can come here—come...home...anytime, day or night. Shorty and I will be here."

He looked at her for a long moment. Then he abruptly stuck the key into his pocket and picked up the duffel bag and went out the door. He walked quickly toward the cab, but another car—one that hadn't been there when he arrived—was parked at the curb. The door on the driver's side opened when he walked by.

"Matt?" someone said, and he spun around.

"Rita, what the hell are you doing here?"

"I got something to say to you, Matt," she said.

"What is it?" he said, not stopping.

"That money you gave me," she called after him. "It's not enough."

Chapter Thirteen

It was much worse than Corey expected. They had never even spent a whole night together, and she felt his absence more acutely than she would have ever believed. She tried to stay busy. She had visits from Santos, whose job it now apparently was to teach her the ins and outs of being a military dependent. And she had been contacted by the lawyer who was handling Matt's petition for custody of the baby. Somehow, Matt had essentially taken care of everything before he left, and all that was left for Corey to do was the simple act of waiting. For the court to set a date and make a ruling. For Matt to come home. She was so afraid for him, so worried. All the time. He had been right. She didn't know how hard it was to be a military wife, even a superficial, marriage-of-convenience one, as she supposedly was.

Someone knocked on the door. Lou Kurian stood on the porch, and Shorty went running to see, looking yet again for the red car at the curb.

"So how's it going?" Lou said when Corey let her in.

"Fine," Corey said, glancing at Lou and then back again because of her expression. "What?"

Lou shook a finger at her. "It *is* that kind of marriage, and don't you try to tell me it's not."

Corey didn't say anything. If it was "that kind," it was completely one-sided.

"So have you heard from him?" Lou asked.

"No. I don't expect to."

"Why not?"

"Because he made a last-minute rule."

"Which was?"

"No letters."

"Yeah, I can see him doing that. He's been a big tough-guy loner for a long time. Letters would be kind of...jarring. Until he gets used to the idea."

"Now, see?" Corey said in exasperation. "You understand that about him right away. Me, I have to have a house fall on me—and I'm supposed to be good at recognizing things like that."

"Well, I have known him a lot longer than you have, and I'm not emotionally involved. But you'll get the hang of it. I'm sure of that."

"Why? Why are you sure of it?"

Lou grinned. "Because it's *that* kind of marriage. So how is our Shorty?"

"She keeps looking for him."

"Sort of like you, huh?"

"Lou—"

"Okay, okay. No more remarks. It's just that I'm…delighted."

"It's a little early in the game for delight."

"Well, there's a reason," Lou said. "Corey, I want things—feelings—to be strong between you and Matt. In the event that you might…need it."

"You're trying to tell me something," Corey said, "and I wish you'd just get to it."

"Rita Warren has asked to see her baby again."

Corey didn't say anything.

"The visit is scheduled for tomorrow," Lou continued. "I need you to bring Shorty in at two."

Corey took a deep breath. "Okay." She could feel how closely Lou was watching her.

"Does Rita…know about Matt and me?" she asked after a moment.

"I don't know. Maybe. The way that squad of his pulled off the wedding is kind of the talk of the post—military tactics and the practical application thereof. And Rita does hang with paratroopers."

Corey looked at her sharply, and Lou shrugged.

"She still gets a supervised visit, Corey."

"I know that. I know she is Shorty's real mother. But I can still be scared, can't I?"

"If you keep it to yourself. Little pictures have big ears—or is it pitchers? Whoa!" Lou said, startled because Shorty ran the big yellow truck she was scooting around on into Lou's ankle. "Doesn't this child have any dolls?" she asked pointedly, and Corey smiled in spite of how little she felt like it.

Lou was looking at her again. "I was wondering how your mom and dad are with all this," she said.

"They're okay, I think. It helped that the neighbors told them the army was trying to hand deliver the wedding invitation. And now that the marriage is a done deed, there's really nothing left to discuss.''

"What about Jacob's mother?"

Corey looked at her. "Jacob's mother is never, ever, going to forgive me."

"I'm sorry."

"It can't be helped. We've had some conversations since the wedding. They were—''

She smiled and looked down, because Shorty had wrapped her arms around Corey's knees for a moment and then was off with the truck again.

I love you, baby girl, she thought. *And I love your father.*

The mailman was coming up the walk, and Corey opened the door to take the letters. Bills. A solicitation from a credit card company. And one letter from S.Sgt. Mateo Beltran.

"What's the matter?" Lou said.

Corey looked at her and held up the envelope. "He said no letters."

"Well, I guess the no-letter rule pertains to you, not to him. I'm going to run along now and let you read that. Tomorrow at two, okay?"

But Corey didn't read it. She sat it on its edge on the mantel where she could see it every time she passed, and she waited until that evening after Shorty had been put to bed, after she had closed the house for the night and taken a long bath. Then and only then, when she was lying in the bed she had briefly shared with Matt did she open his letter.

"So, Madsen," he began. "What's new?" She smiled, both at his use of her former last name and at the teasing question that was nothing if not an understatement. There was quite a bit "new"—in both their lives. She kept reading. It was a "serial" letter, short passages jotted down on different days or different times on the same day.

Talked to an old man this afternoon. He's a retired university professor and his English is really good. He told me about how much he missed the "korzo." That's a kind of walk everybody in the town used to take in the evenings after the work was done. He said it was a time for talking and laughing with your neighbors—or the pretty girls you wanted to impress. The children would run and play. The men would bore each other with their big opinions and the women would gossip, and sometimes there was band music or somebody would start a song and everybody would join in and sing it. But now the people are afraid to come out. A few, maybe, he says still do, but there isn't any joy in it now. He says life isn't worth much without the simple things like the 'korzo'....

Went looking for a secret cache of weapons on this farm. There was nobody there but an old man and his wife. They were afraid of us—not surprising, since we were showing considerable firepower and we weren't exactly invited. They live mostly in one room in this really old fieldstone house. There were strings of red peppers drying all along the walls, beans growing in the garden, but no guns anywhere. I think somebody probably turned their names in for spite.

Ethnic hatred is a fine art in this place. We donated some of our food packs before we left, so I guess they're better off than they were before we got there, even if we did scare the bejesus out of them—that is, if they like pizza....

Somebody here is playing the official anthem of homesick soldiers everywhere. That Elton John song—the one about a military guy leaving his girl behind and how much he loves her. I never paid much attention to it before, but tonight I'm getting the message loud and clear....

I'm tired, Corey. And I'm cold. It's raining again. I wish I had some of your potato soup. No, what I really wish is that I was in bed with you. Okay, I said it, and now I'm going to mail this letter before I change my mind and mark it out. You might as well know how I feel. Kiss Shorty for me.

But he had marked something out after all. She tried to decipher the last line, finally holding it up in front of the lamp. She could make out two of the words—"tell you"—but that was all.

She lay there, holding the letter she couldn't—wouldn't—answer.

After a moment she thought she heard Shorty, and she went to check on her. The baby was still asleep, and Corey stroked her small head and gently pulled the tangled covers off her feet, smiling as she did so. Even at this young age, Shorty had her sleep preferences—at least one set of toes in the open air. She always slept fitfully otherwise. Corey wondered if

Rita Warren even knew that about her baby, that Shorty liked to sleep "barefoot."

But it didn't really matter whether Rita knew or not, or even if she cared. And tomorrow afternoon, she would see her baby for the first time in more than eight months.

Corey walked quietly back to the bedroom. She was still holding the letter, and it occurred to her that it and Shorty were the only things of Matt's she had. He hadn't moved in any of his belongings; he didn't have time. One letter. One baby girl. And the memory of a two-hour honeymoon.

I miss you, she thought as she lay back down. *And I want to tell you so.* She hugged the pillow close to her and closed her eyes, remembering what it had been like with him, the urgency, the not being able to touch enough, kiss enough, be close enough. Had it been the same with Jacob the first time?

No. She really didn't think it had.

She slept better than she would have expected. Shorty awoke at her usual time, but cranky enough not to be interested in her breakfast or much of anything else other than clinging to Corey's neck or knees.

Corey spent most of the morning carrying the baby around, because she couldn't really do otherwise without just walking off and letting her cry.

And she wasn't about to do that. She worked on getting her own emotions in check instead. This baby was *not* going to suffer because Corey couldn't handle today's visit.

She gave Shorty a bath right before it was time

for them to leave, but she didn't dress her up for the reunion with her mother. Just her usual everyday play clothes. Clean play clothes. And shoes that fit.

Don't do that, Corey admonished herself. She didn't know Rita Warren's circumstances, and she had no right to judge her. Corey knew perfectly well that her uncharacteristic need for snideness this morning was because she was so afraid.

She arrived at the Department of Social Services a little early. Lou was waiting for her, and she immediately took a still-fidgety Shorty away with her, leaving Corey to her own devices. As Lou had said the last time Corey had brought the baby in for a supervised visit, she knew the drill.

There were no magazines or books to look at. The waiting area was crowded, as usual, and essentially there was nothing for any of the clientele to do but stare at each other. It was far too hot and humid to go outside, so Corey sat there, trying not to worry and wondering if any of the steady parade of young women arriving and leaving could be Rita Warren.

She kept checking her watch. Finally, when she couldn't stand it any longer, she abruptly got up and walked to a window to look outside—and promptly lost her seat. There was a storm coming up. She could hear a faint rumbling of thunder. She stood and watched the wind blow bits of paper and leaves across the parking lot. The first raindrops began to fall, and a busty young woman with hair that had seen way too much of the curling iron and the bleach bottle ran to stay ahead of the rain. She stopped and looked back at the building once before she got into her car—a car Corey recognized immediately.

Matt's red Corvette.

She stood watching as the woman backed the car around and drove away, absolutely assured that Rita Warren might not have a lot of things, but she certainly had a fine set of wheels.

Matt, now what are you doing?

Corey had no doubt that he was doing something, just as she had no doubt that he clearly had no intention of telling her what that something might be. If he had, there would have been some mention of the Rita-slash-Corvette situation in his letter. And it was her own fault. Anybody who would marry him without being any more informed than *she* had been surely hadn't indicated that she minded being ignorant.

She looked around to see Lou and the baby approaching. Shorty's mouth was turned down in the classic unhappy child face. She was snuffling and there were tears on her cheeks. Children always knew their mothers, just as they knew when they had been abandoned again.

Corey took her, and the baby immediately began crying in earnest.

"Thank God *that's* over," Lou said.

"What happened?" Corey asked, trying to soothe the baby.

"Well, right off the bat I made the mistake of calling Shorty 'Shorty.' Rita took *major* exception to that—her daughter's name was Olivia, and I had damn well better not forget it. Voices were raised—on both sides, I'm sorry to say. Then Shorty started crying and wouldn't stop. She wouldn't have anything to do with Rita or me. *And*—you will be happy to know—as far as Rita Warren is concerned, everything from the crying to the nickname is all *your* fault.''

"She knows about Matt and me," Corey said.

"Exactly. She thinks the two of you are ganging up on her, but she thinks his fascination with you is already on a downward slide and it's only a matter of time before he's available again.''

"Yes, well, she would," Corey said. "She's driving his car.''

Lou frowned. "She's what?''

"Driving his car.''

"The red Corvette!''

"That's the one," Corey assured her.

"Well, how the hell did that happen?''

"Oh, *I* don't know," Corey said, thoroughly vexed now.

"You're sure it's his car?''

"Of course, I'm sure. It's been parked at the curb in front of my house for weeks.''

"All right," Lou said, holding up her hands in mock self-defense. "Just checking, okay? Damn! This doesn't make any sense." She looked at Corey. "Does it?''

Corey sighed instead of answering. She glanced at Shorty, whose mouth was puckering in preparation to cry some more.

"What's the matter, baby girl?" Corey soothed, pressing her face against Shorty's. She felt a little warm, but Corey couldn't tell if it was from the crying or from something more ominous—in which case, she would have more important things to worry about than Rita Warren's mode of transportation.

"Let's blow this joint, okay? We'll go on home, kick back, get us a juice box and watch a little Barney on the television—what do you say?"

Shorty didn't say anything; she cried harder.

"Well, it sounded good to me," Lou said, and Corey smiled.

"I'll see you later," she said. "I'm going home and I'm not going to think about any of this."

"Good luck," Lou said. "I'm going to go sit in a dark room someplace."

It was raining hard by the time Corey drove to the house. She and Shorty both got wet in the dash to the front door. She quickly got the baby into dry clothes and fixed their supper. Shorty ate a little bit of applesauce and drank a few swallows of juice before adamantly refusing anything else. She played halfheartedly with her toys for the rest of the afternoon, and she still cried from time to time, a kind of listless, nonspecific crying that Corey felt like indulging in herself.

"Got to be another tooth," Corey said to reassure herself as much as anything. "That tooth-growing business is tough, baby girl."

She laughed because of the look Shorty gave her.

"Tell you about it, huh?"

She stayed alert for symptoms of some illness, and there were none except for the fretfulness and the lack of appetite. She put Shorty to bed early, rocking her to sleep before she laid her in her crib. Just after three, Corey woke with a start, not because the baby was crying, but because someone was ringing the doorbell. She got up to see, turning on lights as she went. Rita Warren stood on the porch, and she was not happy.

"I want to talk to you," she said without prelude when Corey opened the door.

Corey looked at her, and she didn't pretend that she didn't know who Rita was. "Are you drunk?"

Rita gave a little, chopped off laugh and shook her head. *"No,"* she said pointedly. "I'm not drunk."

"You always do your visiting in the middle of the night?" Corey asked.

"Look! You've got my baby. I want to talk to you, okay? It's...important."

"To whom?"

"Okay, okay!" Rita said. "I get the picture. You're going to jerk my chain and I deserve it—"

The baby began to cry in the other room. "I need to check on Shorty," Corey said, leaving her standing on the porch.

"I wish you'd stop calling her that!" Rita yelled after her. "Hey! I need to tell you something! If *Olivia* is sick, you need to know this, lady!"

Corey came back immediately, carrying the baby. "What is it?"

"She is sick, isn't she?" Rita said, putting both hands on the screen door, trying to see the baby's face.

"Yes," Corey said.

"Let me in. Please."

Corey hesitated for a moment, then unlatched the door.

"Come in. What do you want to tell me?"

Rita reached out to put her hand on Shorty's face.

"God, she's burning up. Didn't you give her anything for it?"

"She didn't have a fever when I put her to bed," Corey said.

"Yeah, well, it looks like you don't know everything, Mrs. Beltran. I could tell she was getting sick. That's why I'm here."

Corey didn't say anything. She took the baby into the kitchen to get the fever reducer for children she kept on hand but had never had to use. Shorty had been sick before—but she'd never had a fever like this.

"Are you going to let me hold her?" Rita asked. "I'm not going to run out the door with her."

Corey looked at her. "I would," she said.

Rita shrugged. "Not if you didn't have anyplace to run *to*. Let me hold her. You need to give her something for the fever quick. I mean it."

Corey handed the baby over. Shorty protested mildly, then laid her head on her mother's shoulder.

"God, she's so big," Rita said. "Hurry up, will you? You want her to have a seizure?"

"What?"

"She gets them if her fever goes up real high, real fast—or so the doctor says. If it's just a little fever, or if it don't come on too quick, you don't have to worry all that much. But I always gave her a dose of that fever medicine when I put her to bed at night if I thought maybe she was coming down with something. So how did you get Matt to marry you?" she asked abruptly.

"I asked him," Corey said, getting the medicine

down from the top shelf in the cabinet. When she turned around, Rita was frowning.

"Damn, I never thought of that. You just *asked* him?"

"Yes," Corey said, filling the medicine dropper carefully.

"Then he fell all over himself saying yes, right?"

"No. He didn't."

That answer seemed to please her. A lot.

"I'll do it," she said, taking the dropper out of Corey's hand and checking the dosage. She gave Shorty the medication, quickly, expertly. "Now I need to show you how to sponge her—"

"I know how to do that."

"Maybe you know how to sponge *a* baby. You don't know how to sponge this one. Do you?"

"Show me," Corey said.

"Okay, then. You don't go putting her in no tub. It scares her and then she cries and her fever goes higher. I need two wet washcloths and a towel—and a rocking chair."

Corey got the things Rita wanted, then took her into the baby's room to the rocking chair that was in there.

"Nice," Rita said, looking around. "Okay, this is how you do it."

Corey watched and learned. And she had to agree. Rita's technique seemed to work quickly with the least aggravation to Shorty.

"See?" Rita said. "That's all you have to do, over and over until it comes down. So is Matt a good daddy or not?" she asked abruptly. "Does he care about Olivia?"

"You know he does," Corey said. "You're driving his car."

"What, you think I hit him up for that?"

"I think you hit him up for something you thought he wouldn't give—so you wouldn't feel so bad about abandoning your little girl."

Rita stared at her. "I don't like you," she said after a moment.

"I don't like you, either," Corey said easily. She was beginning to respect her, but she didn't like her.

"Yeah, well, what the hell. We both sure like *him*, don't we?"

Chapter Fourteen

She's so sick, Corey kept thinking, and the pediatrician wasn't saying anything. Corey waited. Rita, on the other hand, jumped all over her.

"Can you make just a *little* effort, Doctor? I can't read your mind. What's wrong with my kid?"

The doctor overtly gave Corey her undivided attention. "I need to know who has legal custody here."

"I do," Corey and Rita both said. Corey gave her a look.

"Okay, she does," Rita qualified. She stood with her arms folded. Clearly, she didn't intend for that situation to continue for much longer.

"Social Services has actual custody," Corey said. "I'm the foster parent. The baby has been placed with me."

"In that case, Mrs...."

"Beltran," Corey said, and Rita rolled her eyes—more, Corey thought, because the woman had already forgotten her name than because of any continued resentment about the marriage.

"How many times is she going to have to tell you?" Rita said. "Can't you remember anything?"

"Do you want to wait outside?" the doctor asked pointedly.

"No, I don't!" Rita assured her. "Can we get to the bottom line here—or do you get paid by the hour?"

The doctor gave a sharp exhalation of breath. "Mrs. Beltran, this child needs to be admitted to the hospital immediately—"

"What's wrong with her?" Rita demanded.

The pediatrician glanced at her, but she didn't answer the question.

"With her history of febrile convulsions, I think it would be best for her to—"

"What's wrong with her?" Rita said again, her voice rising.

The last thing Corey wanted to do was referee. "She's the baby's mother, Doctor," she said. "We're both worried."

"I understand that. It's just that I'm not used to the noncustodial parent having this much—input."

"Try to get over it," Rita suggested, and Corey gave her another look.

She looked right back. *What?*

"I suspect scarlatina," the pediatrician said. "We've had another case in the last week or so—"

"Could you speak English?" Rita asked no more politely than her previous inquiries.

"Scarlet fever—it's a strep infection, but it's not just a sore throat. Besides that, there is a generalized toxemia—it affects the whole body—"

"How serious is it?" Corey asked.

The doctor looked down at the chart.

"Stop jerking us around," Rita said. "If it's bad, I want to know. *She* wants to know."

The doctor looked up at them. "It's good that you've gotten her here early. We'll put her in the hospital so we can verify whether or not she has the disease. If she does, then it's really a matter of finding the right antibiotic. Until recently, we hardly ever saw a serious case of scarlet fever—and now it seems to be back. It's usually caused by a stronger, mutated strain of beta hemolytic streptococcus. Some of the antibiotics of choice no longer work."

"What does that mean?" Corey asked before Rita could, but it didn't matter. The doctor neatly side-stepped an answer.

"I'm going to get the paperwork done. I want you to wait here with Olivia—both of you. The disease is very contagious. She—and you—need to stay away from the other children in the waiting room."

Corey and Rita looked at each other, and then at Shorty, who was lying so quietly on the examining table. Her face was flushed pink, yet her mouth was so pale.

"I don't know half of what the hell that woman said," Rita said, reaching out to stroke the baby's hair. "Oh, God. Her fever's up again."

Corey stood there, trying to sift through the information about the baby's condition.

It's good you've gotten her here early.

A matter of finding the right antibiotic.

What if they couldn't find it? Or what if they did, but it took too long? She should have asked what happened to the other "case."

Shorty began to cry, holding out her hand for Corey to come to her. Corey leaned over her and kissed her forehead.

"Don't cry, baby face," she said. "I know, I know—this is the pits. First thing we're going to do is feel better, right? Right. And *then*—what will we do? Oh, I know. We'll go to the mall and see the kitty cats. Won't that be good?"

"Kee-kee," Shorty said weakly.

"That's right. Kitty-kitty. A *lot* of kitty-kitties—"

"Corey?" Rita said.

"What?"

"That doctor—there's a whole lot that woman ain't saying."

Corey nodded, because she agreed wholeheartedly and because she didn't trust her voice.

"Corey?" Rita said again. "Are you...scared about this?"

Corey looked at her, remembering suddenly the name this tough young woman had among the paratroopers.

Ready Rita. All she had to do was hear the Rolling Stones singing "Parachute Woman," and old Rita started looking for a pole.

But she wasn't tough or ready right now. She was crying.

Beltran had been out on patrol for days—except that he hadn't been patrolling. He'd been escorting a group of foreign journalists around the so-called safe zones. And he was exhausted from the strain of trying to keep these people—half of whom were women—out of harm's way. They all seemed to think that peacekeeping primarily involved hiding some kind of deep dark secret from their governments. He had never seen such a nutty bunch, and he had no idea what was so hard about the concept of staying out of suspected and uncleared mine fields and booby-trapped houses—even if it did have to be translated from English.

He lost his temper royally once, and he handled it by *not* grabbing one of the men by the back of his belt and hauling him bodily out of a restricted area. He left him out there, and he proceeded to tell him in no uncertain terms that, from now on, he could go wherever the hell he wanted to—they all could, as far as he was concerned—and that the son of a bitch might not have anybody at home who cared if he got his ass blown off, but good old Sergeant Beltran did, and he had no intention of leaving his wife a widow and his baby fatherless or losing any of his soldiers because of some ignorant damn-fool bastard like him. And he made sure the interpreter translated it.

But no matter how exasperated he got, he wasn't allowed to shoot any of them; he just had to endure. By the time they all left, he was determined never to get volunteered for the herd-riding detail again. At least not without a bullwhip. Maybe a big dog.

Now he just wanted to sleep. He didn't want food. He didn't want a shower. He wanted oblivion, for as long as he could get away with it. Naturally, he didn't get anywhere near doing that. He got rerouted to see the first sergeant, who sent him to see the lieutenant, who was new and who didn't have a clue about why Matt was there. The lieutenant left; Matt waited.

And waited.

The lieutenant came back frowning. "Sergeant, you need to pack up your gear."

"Sir?" he said, completely caught off guard. If this was about his decided lack of diplomacy regarding some damned reporter who insisted on tramping around in a mine field, then he expected a verbal reprimand at the very most. He certainly didn't expect to get sent someplace else.

"There's—you have a family emergency."

"Sir, what kind of emergency? Is my wife—"

"I don't have any of the details, Sergeant. All I know is I'm supposed to get you on a transport out of here ASAP. Maybe somebody can tell you something on the other end."

Matt kept standing.

"You'd better hurry, Sergeant, if you're going to make this flight," the lieutenant said, handing him the paperwork. "I'm sorry. I hope everything turns out okay."

God, what's wrong? Matt kept thinking. He felt numb. Dazed. He couldn't think straight. His brain was completely on autopilot. It had to have something to do with Corey or Shorty, or, my God, both of them—

No. Don't even go there. Just get your butt home.

The flight back took forever, and he didn't find out much "on the other end." An airman gave him a ride from the tarmac to the front gate where "somebody" was supposed to pick him up. The somebody turned out to be Lou Kurian.

"Tell me what's wrong," he said as he got into her car. "I don't know a damned thing."

"It's Shorty, Matt. She has scarlet fever. She's very sick. So far the antibiotics they've tried aren't helping. Corey's with her at the hospital."

Scarlet fever.

What did he know about scarlet fever?

Nothing.

"You said 'very sick.' How bad is that?"

"It's—they don't know if she'll make it." He looked at her, and forced himself to take a breath. Then he stared out the window, seeing nothing but the cascade of images in his mind.

The little meat-stick gourmet with the delighted face every time he took another jar out of the grocery bag.

The Merry Mower.

"F'ower—"

"Thanks for coming to get me," he said abruptly before he bawled and couldn't.

"No problem. I knew you didn't have a car." There was just enough emphasis on that last remark for it to penetrate. He glanced at her. "Rita told you," he said. "About the Corvette."

"Nope. Corey did."

He didn't say anything else. He had no wish to get into that now. He just wanted to see his baby.

"Is Shorty going to know who I am?" he asked as Lou slowed the car to let him out at the hospital's front entrance.

"I don't think so, Matt," she said, meeting his eyes.

He sighed heavily and opened the door to get out.

"I'll take your stuff on to Corey's," Lou said. "If I can't get in, I'll leave it with Buck and Carla."

He reached into his shirt and pulled out his dog tags so he could remove the house key Corey had given him. "Here. Take this."

She didn't say anything. She took the key. He thought she was about to say something else, but she didn't, and he was grateful for that. He stared at her for a moment, then gave her a curt nod of thanks. No way could he say it again without losing it.

He used the time it took him to get to the right floor and the right room to focus. He was used to fear. It stood at his elbow every time he jumped, every time he went "peacekeeping." It was there, and he knew it was there. But he never allowed it to interfere with whatever he had to do, and he wasn't going to start now.

He stopped the first nurse-type person he saw. "I'm looking for my wife and baby—"

"Oh, yes," the woman said, looking at his name tag, clearly recognizing who he was. It was a very ominous sign in his experience, arriving at the hospital to see a particular patient and having the staff already know his name.

"This way," she said. "Olivia is in isolation. I'll show you what to do. You'll have to put on a gown before you go in, wear it while you're in there and take it off before you come out, okay?"

"Yeah—how is she?"

"The doctor is on the floor. She's going to see her other patients and then she'll come in and talk to you."

"My wife?"

"I think Corey's in there with Olivia. I'm glad the army let you come home, Sergeant. They both need you."

He stood outside the door, awkwardly trying to get the gown tied so it would stay on. His hands were shaking—he couldn't remember the last time he'd eaten or slept.

The nurse pushed open the door for him, and he went inside. Corey wasn't in there. The nurse stayed, checking the bag of IV fluids and the place on the baby's foot where the needle was inserted. He moved to the side of the bed.

Oh, God, he thought. *Shorty.*

He reached out to touch her hand. Her little chest rose and fell almost as if she were panting. He tried to concentrate on her sweet face, and not on the equipment that surrounded her.

"What's being done for her?" he asked the nurse. His voice cracked, the same way it used to when he was a boy.

"Everything possible," she said. "They've found an antibiotic that this particular strain isn't resistant to, but so far she's not—" She stopped because Shorty opened her eyes. Shorty seemed to want to cry and couldn't. It broke his heart.

"Is it all right if I—can I talk to her?" he asked, and the nurse nodded.

He moved closer, leaning down so that she could hear him. "Hey, Short Stuff," he said softly. "It's me. How are you doing, huh?" He gently caressed her face.

She stirred again, and he looked at the nurse.

"It's okay. Go ahead," she said.

"Hey, baby," he continued. "Hey, Shorty—are you going to open your eyes for me a little bit here? Shorty…"

He heard the door open behind him, and he turned to look. Rita stood there in the same kind of paper gown, her face pale and unreadable.

She shrugged. "Yeah, I know," she said. "What a surprise."

As far as he was concerned, that remark was the height of understatement. He had never even considered the possibility that she would be here. He hadn't even considered the possibility that she'd still be in the state. The last he heard, it was open-audition time at the Vegas clubs again, a biannual event for aspiring exotic dancers everywhere, and Rita was happily on her way to the big time—with most of his money and all of his car.

No wonder Corey knew about the Corvette, he thought. How was he going to explain that? He knew

Corey well enough to know that as much as she cared about his kid, she wouldn't want him trying to buy Rita off. And that was essentially what he'd done. The only problem was, like most bribes, clearly it didn't take.

"Don't look at me like that, Matt," Rita said. "Don't look at me like you think I've got no business being here!"

"Rita—"

"Excuse me," the nurse said. "Maybe you two would like to take this outside?"

Fine, he thought. He was *not* going to get into some kind of big drama queen thing with Rita. Not now and not here. He glanced at the nurse, then turned his attention back to Shorty for a moment, kissing her lightly on her forehead before he went. He took charge and pointed Rita toward the door, but he had never felt so helpless in his life.

"Matt," Rita said as soon as they were out in the hall. "Don't be mean to me. Please—"

"Rita, I'm not being mean to you."

Tears were rolling down her face, and she leaned against him. He put his arm around her shoulders, wondering where Corey had gone.

"Take it easy," he said after a moment, making her look at him. "This isn't going to help."

"You're wrong. It does help." She hid her face against his chest again. "This is not working out the way I planned," he thought he heard her say.

She looked up at him. "I wanted you to get to know your kid," she continued. "That's why I left her—"

"Hey," he said. "It's me, remember? Not Bugs and not Burke. I know what the deal is here. You had a chance to get to Las Vegas in time for the dance auditions. And you couldn't be bothered with a baby. And that's where you'd be now if she hadn't gotten so sick even *you* couldn't go off and leave her—"

"I wanted you to love her!"

"I do," he said. More than either of them would have ever suspected.

They stared at each other; she looked away first.

"So you've been here at the hospital with Corey the whole time?" he asked.

"Yeah."

"How did that happen? I know Lou wouldn't okay the two of you becoming new best friends."

"I went to see *her* after you left," she said, lifting her chin and smiling. "I went in the middle of the night. Boy, she was angry, but she's such a damn *lady,* she wouldn't dare show it. And Shorty was already getting sick, so she couldn't turn me away. You and me, we used to laugh about prissy women like her—remember?"

"Don't," he said.

"Don't what?"

"I told you how it was with me before I left. I gave you everything I had. I don't have any more money. I don't have anything you want."

"What did you go and get married for, Matt? Huh? If you'd just waited until I got a few things straight, you and me could have—"

"No, Rita," he said. "We couldn't."

"You don't even know that woman!"

"I know all I need to know."

"How did you two get so tight? That's what I want to know."

"You did that."

"What do you mean?"

"You made it happen, Rita. We never would have even met if you hadn't left Shorty in my car like that."

"Don't call her that stupid name!" she cried, causing several people who were standing at the end of the hall to turn and stare. "Her name is Olivia! Olivia!"

"Look! I don't know why we're going around and around about any of this. Can't you see how sick that little girl is? You and I both know what your priorities are. Now I'm going back inside to be with our daughter. Maybe you want to come with me."

She didn't. He was both relieved and annoyed. He sat for a long time beside Shorty's bed. Talking to her. Coaxing her into taking swallows of juice from a straw after the nurse showed him how.

There was a time or two when Shorty opened her eyes that he thought she might know who he was.

And he kept waiting for Corey to return.

Where the hell was she?

The doctor came and went. Matt tried to comprehend at least some of what the woman had said. As far as he could tell, the medical profession was doing everything it was supposed to do and everything it could do—but nobody had any idea whether or not it was enough.

Someone else came in.

"Sorry to disappoint you," Rita said when he looked around. "If you're looking for your *wife*, she left."

"What do you mean, she left?"

"I can't make it any plainer than that. Olivia's got her real mother to look after her. I guess the woman figured she didn't have to hang around here anymore, so she cut out."

"She wouldn't do that."

"No? Well, you haven't seen her around, have you? I think she's had all the motherhood she can stand."

"Rita—"

"Maybe you want to cut out, too. Who needs you here, anyway? What a joke—you really think Olivia is yours, don't you? Well, she's not!"

He didn't say anything. He didn't trust himself to utter even one word. He was way too tired and too worried to play this game.

But Rita wasn't about to let it go. She had made her big announcement, and now she was going to go down with both guns blazing.

"What? You don't believe me? It's true. I lied to you, Matt. I *lied*. She's not yours!"

"Rita, I took the paternity test. I *am* that baby's father. Can't you ever tell the truth?"

She looked at him. She had forgotten that small likelihood. But she wasn't finished.

"Yeah, I can tell the truth, Matt. I told Corey the truth."

Someone else was about to come into the room.

He could hear the rattle of a cart or something outside.

"I told her the truth about her husband," Rita said anyway. "Not you, Matt. Her *other* husband. I told her the truth about Jacob."

"What are you talking about?"

The door opened. Rita smiled. "I knew Jacob Madsen. You understand what I'm saying?"

"Sergeant, we're going to be doing some things in here for a little while," the nurse said.

He looked at her blankly, tearing his attention away from Rita's triumphant face.

"The lab is going to draw some more blood, and then we're going to give Olivia a bath, change her bed and her gown. Why don't you go stretch your legs? Maybe go get something to eat."

"Yeah, okay," he said. "Have you seen my wife?" he asked abruptly.

"I think she already left," the nurse said.

Rita gave him an arch look. She had no idea that her revelation only confirmed what he already knew about the woman he had married. If she wasn't here, then there was a damned good reason.

He kissed Shorty, then he left the room and stood in the hallway for a moment to get his bearings. He looked at his watch—a mostly unhelpful gesture. It was still set on Balkan time, and his brain simply wouldn't do the math. He understood exactly what Rita was doing. Old dreams died hard. She was a long, *long* way from becoming a showgirl, and the contingency plan she'd put together for herself—and him—had completely fallen through. He understood all of that, and for a little while there, he had even felt sorry for her. But right now, he was ready to wring her neck. He had to find Corey. Corey wouldn't understand the one basic truth about the Ritas and the Burkes of this world. It was another of Father Andrew's axioms.

Some people lie when they don't have to.

He began an immediate search of the perimeter, checked with whatever personnel he could find. Nobody had seen Corey lately, and nobody could verify that she had actually left the building, regardless of what Rita and the nurse had said.

He tried calling the house.

No answer.

He checked the lobby, the snack shop, the grounds, the parking lot, the sidewalks.

No Corey.

He called the house again. Still no answer. He stood there, trying not to worry. She drove crazy when she was upset and by herself in a car. He knew that firsthand.

When he crossed the lobby yet another time, he ran into Shorty's pediatrician. She was actually smiling.

"Sergeant Beltran," she said. "I think I have a little good news for you."

He looked at her. "I could use some," he said.

"I just got Olivia's last lab report. Things are looking better."

"You're sure?"

"I'm sure."

"Why is the lab report better—but she isn't?"

"Well, it takes time, Sergeant. The improvement in her blood work is a good indicator of things to come."

A good indicator, he thought. He could use some of those, too.

He went back to the room, but according to someone in the hallway, the bath and bed change was still in progress. He didn't see Rita anywhere.

He started walking back toward the elevators, with no plan in mind, except perhaps to call Lou. The doors opened just as he got there, and Corey got off. She saw him immediately. Her hand flew to her mouth, but she didn't come to him. She stood there, trying not to cry, holding a kitten book with the sales slip sticking out of it. She looked so tired, and so beautiful.

"We need to talk," he said, taking her by the arm.

"Shorty—is she—" she began in alarm.

"No, the doctor says her lab work is better—whatever the hell that means. They're giving her a bath now. Let's go outside." He turned her around and guided her back onto the elevator, not giving her time to decline the invitation. She kept looking at him on the way down, but at least she didn't refuse.

Outside, the afternoon was hot and humid. He could see thunderheads to the northwest. There were a few park benches around, but they were already taken. He walked Corey to a low stone wall, to a spot in the shade, then, without asking, he lifted her up so she could sit on it.

He took the kitten book out of her hands and laid it aside. "Look at me," he said.

She did as he asked, but she wasn't finding it easy.

"You can't believe everything Rita tells you."

"About Jacob, you mean?"

He looked into her eyes. "Yeah. About Jacob."

She gave him a sad smile. "She knew him."

"Corey, no, she didn't. She's just—"

"Rita called him once—at home. You were there."

He frowned, then remembered. Carla Rafferty coming to get Corey to talk to someone on the phone, someone who was so upset because she hadn't known that Jacob Madsen had died.

"You aren't going to get all crazy about this and start thinking Rita had something with Jacob, are you?" he said. He was as worldly as they came, and he had never even met Jacob Madsen, but he did know Rita, and he was not about to suspend his disbelief.

"Well, she met him somewhere. He did some group counseling for the court system." She abruptly smiled. "He did group counseling in the produce aisle at the grocery store or the bus stop if he got the chance. It's the way he was—the bringer of lambs into the fold. But he's gone and I'm pretty much stuck with whatever Rita wants me to think. It's got me second guessing everything."

"Corey—"

"I can't talk about this with you."

"Why not?" he said, surprised at how offended he was by the remark. "You think I'm too damn dumb to understand how much this hurts you?"

"Jacob and Rita are not the problem. *I* am the problem. And you."

"Meaning what?"

"Meaning I can't keep my part of the bargain."

"Are you telling me you want out of the marriage? Is that where this is going—" He stopped because of the way she was looking at him.

"I love you so much," she said.

"What?"

"Matt, aren't you paying attention?" she said in exasperation. Her mouth trembled.

"I…yes—*yes*. You said you…love me."

She nodded. And quickly wiped away the tear that slid down her cheek with the heel of her hand.

"Why is *that* a problem?" he asked. "It's not a problem—"

"Yes, it is. It's only going to make you unhappy. I'll hang all over you—the way I did with Jacob."

"Maybe I want you to hang all over me," he said. He ignored the passerby who overheard the remark and who approved the concept heartily.

"No, you don't. You're the big tough-guy loner. I can't do things your way," she said, reaching up to briefly touch the side of his face. "I thought I could, but I can't. And I know I can't. I understand that you need your space. I even understand why. But I'll never be able to give it to you, not feeling about you the way I do. I'll make you miserable."

"Corey—"

"Don't you see? It would be terrible for you and for me. Most of all, it would be terrible for Shorty."

He kept looking at her, trying to understand.

"So what are you going to do? Bail out now when she needs you? When I need you? Am I just supposed to hand her over to Rita because it got too complicated for you emotionally? What if Shorty doesn't make it? How am I supposed to get through something like that without you—" He stopped, because he was going to bawl if he didn't. He tried to move away. She caught his hand to keep him there.

But she didn't say anything.

"When we got married, I meant the words," he said. "But if you think it's not going to work with us, then it won't. Forget what I just said. I'm not going to use Shorty to make you stay where you don't want to be—no matter how much I might want to—"

"Sergeant Beltran?" someone said from behind him.

He looked around, immediately recognizing one of the hospital volunteers. "Yeah?" he said.

"They need you to come back to the pediatric floor."

His eyes locked with Corey's. "Do you know why?" he asked the volunteer.

"No, Sergeant."

He helped Corey off the wall and handed her the kitten book. They went quickly, taking the stairs instead of the elevator. He didn't see anyone in the hallway when they came out of the stairwell. He didn't see anyone until he threw open the isolation room door.

Shorty was sitting up in the middle of the crib.

Her hair had been brushed and she was wearing a little pink barrette.

"Boo!" she said, clapping her hands together. *"Boo!"*

He struggled for control. The best day and the worst day of his life, he thought. He had his daughter again; Shorty was going to be all right.

But he'd lost Corey.

Chapter Fifteen

"So how's the baby?" Lou asked.

"Good as new," Corey said. "Except her skin is still peeling. And some days she runs a little fever in the afternoon."

"And your husband?" Lou persisted.

She didn't answer.

"This is not just an idle question," Lou said. "This is more a social worker question. If you get my drift."

"He's staying at the barracks for two more days, then he's leaving."

"Uh-huh," Lou said, writing in the stenographer's notebook she carried. "Staying at the barracks. Leaving in two days. Be gone for about six months. Marriage all shot to hell—"

Corey looked at her, but she still didn't say anything.

"I'm waiting," Lou said.

"Okay, fine! You were absolutely right!"

"I was right? That's all you've got to say?"

"What do you want to hear?"

"I want to hear that you and Beltran are going to get with the program—that's what I want to hear. *I* was right! What kind of malarkey is that? I wasn't right—I was *wrong!* You and Beltran should be together—here—and you're not. You are both completely nuts."

"Thank you," Corey said.

"I mean it! You took a perfectly promising marriage, and what did you do with it? I am so aggravated. With you especially. You love the man. You love his child. You're a great mother and a great wife. Why isn't this thing working, Corey? Talk to me here!"

"There's nothing to talk about."

"No? What about Rita?"

"Rita loves her child a lot more than I ever suspected."

"Oh. So you've had some kind of revelation here, and now you think it's okay for Shorty to go live in a topless bar."

"Lou, I am trying to do the best thing for Shorty."

"And the best thing *isn't* living in a stable home with her father and you, the people who love her? Corey, I do not understand this situation."

"Matt understands it—"

"No, he doesn't," he said from the porch. He

opened the screen door and came inside. "Hey, Lou."

"Hey, yourself," she said, still cranky.

Corey tried not to stare at him. It wasn't easy; she hadn't seen him in almost two weeks. Supposedly, he had to stay away from Shorty until she was no longer contagious and until the incubation period was over and the medical officer could be sure he was fit for duty. He had just had a haircut—one of those military, buzz-cut things. And he looked...adorable.

"I *don't* understand the situation," he said.

"Yes, you do."

"No, I don't. I don't," he repeated to Lou. "So tell me—and Lou—why it isn't working?"

"Because it's all one-sided, for one thing," she said, bending to pick up some of Shorty's toys off the floor.

"How is it one-sided if we love each other?" he asked.

"We don't love each other. *I* love you. Period."

"Well, I love you, too," he said.

She looked at him. "Since when?"

"Since when? Since...probably the day I bawled you out for running a red light. And you said as long as I was here, I should come in and see Shorty— because you knew that's why I was here in the first place, but you let me save face and you didn't give me any grief about it."

She looked at him. "You love me, too," she said, trying to understand.

"Roger that," he said.

She gave a sharp sigh. "Matt, you are the one who said love is no good reason for a marriage."

"Okay, so I made a sweeping generalization. The trouble with those things is that there's some kind of...cosmic committee somewhere just waiting for you to say something idiotic like that so it can cut you off at the knees. And believe me, the committee definitely heard me. Corey, how could you not know how I feel about you? Lou knew—didn't you, Lou?"

"Absolutely," Lou said helpfully.

"Matt, you never *said*."

"Yes, I did."

"When!"

"At the wedding. Didn't I okay the love and honor part? And I said it at the hospital—when we went outside to talk."

"I'm the one who said it. *You* said it wasn't a problem."

"Well, that's why it wasn't a problem—because I love you, too."

"You didn't tell me any of that."

He frowned. "Then I...guess communication is something I need to work on."

"Yes, I guess it is."

The three of them stared at each other.

"Well!" Lou said abruptly. "Where is our Shorty again?"

"In the den watching the dinosaur," Corey said, looking into Matt's eyes.

"I think I'll go watch with her. Maybe close this door? I do love that big old purple creature. We wouldn't want to disturb you."

She left and shut the door firmly behind her.

Corey stood still, not knowing what to say. Matt came closer, but he made no attempt to touch her. His eyes moved over her face.

"Nothing's changed," she began. "You're still—"

"You take my breath away," he interrupted quietly. "Every time I look at you, I...ache with loving you. I love being with you and talking to you...making love with you. God, I love making love with you. I wasn't ready for any of this. You know that. I didn't want to be a father, and I sure as hell didn't want to be a husband. But what you don't know—what I've been afraid to tell you—is how much I need you. You and Shorty are everything to me. I think I've been waiting for you my whole life, and I wish—"

He stopped.

"What?" she asked.

"I wish I could come to you without so many problems. This thing with Rita is going to drag on, and you're the one who will have to deal with it, because I won't be here half the time. Being married to me isn't going to be anything like what you had with Jacob. I am so jealous of him—you didn't know that, either, did you? I don't know what to do about it and that's probably going to get in the way. Your mom and dad—just about everybody who cares about you—think you've made a big mistake getting hooked up with somebody like me. Hell, even *I* think you've made a mistake. But what I told you before is the truth. I meant the words when we got married. I *meant* them, damn it!''

He came closer, and he put his hands on her shoulders. She leaned against him, closing her eyes as his arms slid around her. She loved him so much!

''I don't have anything to give you,'' he said. ''Except myself.''

''That's enough.''

''Is it?''

''It was always enough.''

''It's going to be rough sometimes.''

''I know.''

''We could start over, if you want. Get married again when I get back.''

''No, I think the first one took.''

''Don't you want something a little more…sane?''

''No, I'd rather have you,'' she said, and he chuckled softly.

''Too easy, Madsen,'' he whispered. ''Too easy.''

Epilogue

Corey saw Meyerhauser first. He came bounding up
on the porch to hold open the door.

"Now it's not as bad as it looks," he assured her.

"What? Oh!"

She saw Matt coming up the sidewalk. He was
walking—but just barely. He had one knee in some
kind of brace and one hand and arm bandaged.

She grabbed Shorty to keep her from running at
him, and stood back out of the way.

"Meyerhauser, what happened?" she asked, because she knew she wouldn't get much out of Matt.

"Well, you know those Flying Elvises and people
like that that who do those fancy jumps at fairs and
mall openings?"

"Yes."

"And when they land, it's so soft it's just like stepping off a curb?"

"Yes," she said again.

"The sergeant's landing—it wasn't *nothing* like that," he said.

"That'll be fine, Meyerhauser," Matt said pointedly as he struggled up the steps. "Hey, baby," he said to her, stopping long enough to kiss her on the eyebrow and Shorty on the fist.

"Are you all right?" she asked worriedly.

"Yeah. Why?" He changed his mind about going inside and began hobbling in the direction of the porch swing instead.

"*Why?* How about because you had to be carried home on your shield?"

"No, I'm walking. See?"

"Yes, I see. That's the problem."

"They wanted to keep him overnight, but he talked them out of it," Meyerhauser said helpfully.

"Meyerhauser—" Matt sat down heavily on the swing, and Meyerhauser dragged up a wicker chair for him to prop his leg on.

"You don't have to worry, ma'am," Meyerhauser said. "If he wasn't mostly all right, he couldn't have talked them out of nothing."

"Owie," Shorty said, looking at her father's bandaged arm. She patted him gently on his nonbraced knee. "Poor, poor," she said sadly.

"Come up here, Short Stuff," he said, lifting her up with his good hand. "I need a hug. Give me the best one you got."

She hugged him and threw in a kiss as well.

"All right! One more time! Now I'm in good shape."

"Good sape," she told him, climbing back down to go get her wagon and pull it along the sidewalk.

"Meyerhauser, you know what to do," Matt said.

"Yes, Sergeant. Everything is under control, Sergeant." He turned to go, then came back up the steps. "You better have this, ma'am," he said to Corey, handing her a card.

"Thank you for bringing him home," she said.

"Nothing to it, ma'am—if you don't mind swearing. Oh, my virgin ears!"

"That'll be *fine,* Meyerhauser," Matt said again.

Meyerhauser grinned. "You hold it in the road, Shorty," he said, stepping over her and the wagon as he left.

Corey looked down at the card he had given her. It was full of telephone numbers.

Matt reached out and made her sit down on the swing beside him. He shifted painfully until he had made enough room for her to lean against his good side. They sat there, watching Shorty climb in and out of her wagon.

"Everybody okay?" he whispered in her ear.

"Very okay," she said. She was still surprised by her pregnancy—that it had happened on their two-hour honeymoon and that there had been no complications of any kind. That is, if she didn't count Matt's anger that she had waited awhile to tell him. She had thought it would be better not to give him something else to worry about while he was in the Balkans. He thought otherwise. And said so. By excluding him, she had hurt his feelings and his pride, and, suffice it to say, she wouldn't make *that* mistake again.

"Are you sure you're all right?" she asked, turning so she could see his face. Her eyes held his. It could have been a lot worse, and they both knew it.

"I just got the bark knocked off and I can't walk so good, that's all. So how was *your* day?"

"Rita was here, that's how it was," she said. "And Evangeline."

He shook his head. "What did our Rita want?"

"She said she just wanted to see Shorty for a little while, but that wasn't it."

"What then—money?"

"No, she wanted to talk."

"About what?"

"About Jacob."

"She didn't start that stuff again—"

"No, she just wanted to tell me how she knew him and why she called here and asked for him that day. She wasn't in one of his groups, but she had a friend who was. The friend gave Rita Jacob's name. Rita said she knew she'd done a really bad thing, abandoning Shorty the way she did, and she needed somebody to talk to. It took her a long time to get up the nerve to call him, and then when she found out the only person who could supposedly help her had died, she just…lost it. Bugs must have talked her into finally telling me what happened. He came with her. I think he's in love with her."

"What about Evangeline? I hope to God they weren't both here at the same time."

She laughed. "No, they missed each other by several seconds. Evangeline…didn't know I was pregnant."

"I take it she was thrilled."

Corey didn't say anything. He didn't need to know just how unthrilled Jacob's mother had been. She reached up to touch his face. "Evangeline still needs me to grieve with her, that's all. And she doesn't want to believe that I don't have to do that anymore. It doesn't mean that I didn't love Jacob. It just means that I've moved on and I'm making a new life—with you."

"You're sure you're okay? The baby's okay?"

"I'm fine. And the baby is as rowdy as ever—here, feel."

She put his hand where the baby had just kicked.

"Hey, Matt!" Buck called from across the street. "What happened to you!"

"I misplaced the ground, Buck!" he called back, and the old man laughed.

"Carla just baked some cookies," he called. "She wants to know can we borrow Shorty for a little bit? We need a taste-tester."

"Just send the extras home with her," Matt said.

"Ain't going to be no extras, boy. What's wrong with you?"

Buck came and got the baby. They walked hand in hand back across the street, Shorty looking up at him and talking all the way.

"Mom and Dad are coming by to pick her up this evening," Corey said. "Mom thinks I need to rest up these last few days."

"You mean you and I are going to be in the house *alone?* All night?"

"That's what I mean."

"Oh!" he said, shifting his weight on the swing. "Damn, that hurts." He gave a heavy sigh. "Well—oh! We could play cards, I guess."

"No, we couldn't. I have to go to the bathroom every two minutes and you'd cheat while I'm gone."

"Would not."

"Would, too. You like to win too much."

"You don't go into any situation thinking you might lose, Madsen."

"Is that so?" she asked, smiling into his eyes.

He became serious suddenly. "Corey, you know I love you, don't you? If I don't say it enough, it's not because I—"

She kissed him, a long lingering kiss that belied their mutually taxed physical conditions.

"Speaking of cards," she said abruptly. She held up the one with all the telephone numbers. "What is this?"

"Contingency plans."

"For what?"

"For your transportation. When you go into labor."

"I don't understand."

"I can't drive. I can't bend my knee," he said. "Shorty doesn't know how—even if she wasn't staying at your mother's. And what with labor pains and water breaking, you might be too busy to operate a motor vehicle. The squad will take care of it."

"Is this the same squad that did the wedding?"

"Pretty much," he said. "Why? You can trust them. They'll get you there."

"Oh, I know," she said, smiling. "I just don't think all those people are going to fit into the delivery room, that's all."

He laughed and kissed her hard and well.

"So what have you got to say about *that?*" he teased, infinitely pleased with himself because he'd caught her off guard and because Buck had whistled appreciatively from all the way across the street.

She smiled into his eyes, delighting in the love she saw there.

"I say...Go, Airborne!"

* * * * *

Silhouette

SPECIAL EDITION

™
That's My Baby!

Don't miss these heartwarming stories coming to
THAT'S MY BABY!—only from
Silhouette Special Edition®!

June 1998   LITTLE DARLIN'
by Cheryl Reavis (SE# 1177)

When cynical Sergeant Matt Beltran found an abandoned
baby girl that he might have fathered, he turned to compassionate foster mother Corey Madsen. Could the healing
touch of a tender family soothe his soul?

August 1998   THE SURPRISE BABY
by Nikki Benjamin (SE# 1189)

Aloof CEO Maxwell Hamilton married a smitten Jane Elliott
for the sake of convenience, but an impulsive night of
wedded bliss brought them a surprise bundle of joy—and a
new lease on love!

October 1998 FATHER-TO-BE
by Laurie Paige (SE# 1201)

Hunter McLean couldn't exactly recall fathering a glowing
Celia Campbell's unborn baby, but he insisted they marry
anyway. Would the impending arrival of their newborn
inspire this daddy-to-be to open his heart?

THAT'S MY BABY!
Sometimes bringing up baby can bring surprises...
and showers of love.

Available at your favorite retail outlet.

Take 2 bestselling love stories FREE

Plus get a FREE surprise gift!

Special Limited-Time Offer

Mail to Silhouette Reader Service™

3010 Walden Avenue
P.O. Box 1867
Buffalo, N.Y. 14240-1867

YES! Please send me 2 free Silhouette Special Edition® novels and my free surprise gift. Then send me 6 brand-new novels every month, which I will receive months before they appear in bookstores. Bill me at the low price of $3.57 each plus 25¢ delivery and applicable sales tax, if any.* That's the complete price, and a saving of over 10% off the cover prices—quite a bargain! I understand that accepting the books and gift places me under no obligation ever to buy any books. I can always return a shipment and cancel at any time. Even if I never buy another book from Silhouette, the 2 free books and the surprise gift are mine to keep forever.

235 SEN CH7W

Name	(PLEASE PRINT)
Address	Apt. No.
City	State	Zip

This offer is limited to one order per household and not valid to present Silhouette Special Edition® subscribers. *Terms and prices are subject to change without notice. Sales tax applicable in N.Y.

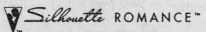

The World's Most Eligible Bachelors are about to be named! And Silhouette Books brings them to you in an all-new, original series....

World's Most Eligible Bachelors

Twelve of the sexiest, most sought-after men share every intimate detail of their lives in twelve never-before-published novels by the genre's top authors.

Don't miss these unforgettable stories by:

Dixie Browning

MARIE FERRARELLA

Jackie Merritt

Tracy Sinclair

BJ James

RACHEL LEE   Suzanne Carey

Gina Wilkins

VICTORIA PADE

MAGGIE SHAYNE   *Anne McAllister*

Susan Mallery

Look for one new book each month in the **World's Most Eligible Bachelors** series beginning September 1998 from Silhouette Books.

Available at your favorite retail outlet.

MATERNITY LEAVE

Coming September 1998

Three delightful stories about the blessings
and surprises of "Labor" Day.

TABLOID BABY by Candace Camp

She was whisked to the hospital in the nick of time....

THE NINE-MONTH KNIGHT
by Cait London

A down-on-her-luck secretary is experiencing
odd little midnight cravings....

THE PATERNITY TEST by Sherryl Woods

The stick turned blue before her
biological clock struck twelve....

*These three special women are very pregnant...and very
single, although they won't be either for too much longer,
because baby—and Daddy—are on their way!*

Available at your favorite retail outlet.